STRANGE GATEWAYS

STRANGE GATEWAYS

SIMON KURT UNSWORTH

DIP

Design & Layout by Michael Smith
Printed and bound in England by T. J. Books

PS Publishing Ltd
Grosvenor House, 1 New Road
Hornsea, HU18 1PG. England

editor@pspublishing.co.uk   www.pspublishing.co.uk

CONTENTS

FOREWORD VII

MORRIS EXPEDITION, DAYS NINE AND TEN 3

F BOMB 11

THE HOTEL GUEST 27

THE KNITTED CHILD 45

THE DRINKS' TOTEM 55

IMPLEMENTING THE LEAST DESIRABLE SOLUTION 69

TRAFFIC STREAM 87

A MAN OF ICE AND SORROW 99

MAMI WATA 115

THE SEVEN PEOPLE YOU DON'T MEET TODAY 139

PEEK A BOO 157

COEL COETH 165

AFTERWORD 193

STORY NOTES 197

ACKNOWLEDGEMENTS 211

FOREWORD

THERE'S A TEMPTATION to rewrite things when you republish them. You can use your extra years of writing to improve the stories, you can remove people from the acknowledgements who've pissed you off or who you're divorced from or who you've just decided you don't like any more and no longer deserve your beneficence. It's like being God, only pettier... but pettiness helps no one in the long run and God had probably better take a more charitable approach to these things. So, the bulk of this collection remains the same as it's always been, warts and all. If I'm no longer in contact with all the people in the acknowledgements it doesn't matter. They were important to me then, even if not now.

In rereleasing *Strange Gateways* there are new people to thank though: PS (again!) for still having faith in the work, the now near-adult boy Ben (a fine author in his own right) for still being my best creation and my mate Seb for the swimming and the movie nights. This collection remains dedicated to Rosie, though, for now and for ever. I'm still looking at you holding that tea on the slope in the sun and wondering how I got so lucky.

A note: "Coel Coeth" was a submission written for a Halloween anthology that was rejected because the anthology was being produced by a US publisher and my Wales-set tale wasn't American enough. So, as they say, goes life. It's a story I enjoyed writing, and I hope you enjoy reading. I have literally no idea how to pronounce its title though.

—Simon Kurt Unsowrth
August 2022

True love, have you bought me gold?
Or silver to set me free?
For to save my body from the cold, cold ground
and my neck from the gallows tree?

Prickle-Eye Bush, trad.

MORRIS EXPEDITION, DAYS NINE AND TEN

"**H**ERE?"
"Here."
"He's sure?"
"Yes."

Morris nodded and turned, blocking Tunney, the translator, out. He checked his camera again, wiping condensation from the lens with his sleeve. Looking through its distancing eye, the trees and foliage were a lush green, sharply delineated.

"You remember the deal?" asked the guide through Tunney.

"Of course," said Morris. "You bring us here. You get paid. You leave before nightfall."

"Before late afternoon," said Tunney. "He says it does not always wait for night, that it comes before nightfall or in the night as it wants to, and he wants to be gone before then. Before it discovers that you are here, if it does not know already. Before it *hunts*."

"Better go then," said Morris. "We're here, and the day's

3

getting on." He ignored the rest of the conversation between Tunney and the guide, a chatter like the monkeys in the zoo Morris had visited as a child. Instead, he turned his gaze to the slope below him.

He looked on, approving, taking in all the activity bustling around him. The camp was springing up smoothly, like watching a time-lapse film of a new city emerging from the ground; perimeter cameras on tripods, a communications centre, a latrine, tents, fires over which dangled blackened cooking pots. And, of course, there was Bailey, overseeing it all, pointing and laughing, and having fun. Even after nine days of hot, uncomfortable travel and false starts, of frustrating failure, he was bright and cheerful. Nothing phased the man and Morris, knowing it was churlish but not caring, hated him for it.

Morris moved down into the cluster of tents, looking for his own. It was half-erected, the canvas billowing and flapping around the tubular skeleton as the men inside it moved around. His bags were on the ground next to the tent, and he was annoyed to see that one had spilled over, was letting loose a drift of his clothes and papers. He went to retrieve them and realised, to his further irritation, that the guide and Tunney had followed him and were still talking.

"He says that you should leave," said Tunney.

Morris stopped what he was doing and looked over at the guide. Astonishingly, the man looked upset; he was twisting his ridiculous hat between his hands and speaking in a fast stream of unintelligible local dialect. Tunney nodded, and Morris was glad to see that even he looked uncomfortable, was struggling to keep up with the ever-increasing flow of glottal stops and run-on consonants that rose in pitch the longer the guide spoke. He was adding gestures into the mix now, his arms flinging wide as he pointed at the forest and then jabbing his hand back the way they had come, to the scrubland and distant plain.

"He says this is a cursed place," said Tunney finally, a worried look playing across his face like a ripple across the surface of a lake. "That the thing you seek is a curse made flesh and that it will surely destroy you as it has destroyed those that came before you. That it moves in silence and eats at leisure. It steps between the trees like a ghost. It cannot be seen until the moment it strikes and it will devour those who come to search for it. He says we should go before it is too late."

Morris waved a dismissive hand. He knew about the rumours and the earlier expeditions, about Cathcart's disastrous hunting trip, Jackson's photograph of something blurred and huge in the woods and the missing geological surveyors, Clifton and Willets. They, and every other strange sighting and missing prospector, had *brought* Morris here after trying all those other places in the last nine days. All the triangulated data, eyewitness accounts excavated from dusty files and police records and pamphlets and out-of-print books; they had all led him here. It was his last chance of success before the money was pulled, although he had neither the time nor the inclination to explain this to the guide, so instead he simply said to Tunney, "Thank him for his concern. Tell him we are very well equipped, and if he's happy with his payment, he can go."

Once the message was relayed, the guide let loose with another string of shouted invocations, his arms wild and his hat flapping in his hand. Morris merely nodded, letting a 'thank you, we're done here' smile play across his face. The guide, seeing he was getting nowhere, finally turned and walked quickly back along the trampled path and into the trees.

"He seemed very insistent," said Tunney.

"He was probably after more money," said Morris. "They normally are."

Once the camp was set up, they carried out an exploratory scout. Morris' instincts had led them correctly; this was an ideal environment. The heavy foliage around the camp carried on for perhaps two miles before thinning again, giving way to a grassy scrub and eventually the lakeshore. Wildlife trails shifted and danced between the trees, most leading down to the lake, although none looked big enough to hold the thing they sought. Returning to the camp at nightfall, they had found no sign of it. Still, Morris thought, it was optimistic to think they might have come across evidence on the first exploration of the area.

A delegation of the bearers came to Morris' tent in the morning, led by Tunney. One of them held a hat that Morris recognised but could not, at first, place. Tunney, nervous, said, "They found the hat while getting water this morning."

"Holy shit!" said Morris, suddenly remembering where he had seen it before. "It's the guide's!"

"They're concerned," said Tunney. "They think something has happened to him and want to search."

"No," said Morris immediately. "It's taken us far longer to get here than we first anticipated and we haven't much time. Besides, he probably just dropped it."

"It was found by the lakeshore," said Tunney. "In the opposite direction to the one he went off in."

"Maybe he went for a drink," said Morris, but even he didn't believe it. *By God*, he thought suddenly, *another one taken, another disappearance!* They couldn't have been luckier unless they stumbled over the thing having a nap!

"Tell them we'll look for him while we look for the creature. We'll start by the lake, where the hat was found."

Tracks. There would be fresh tracks, and spores. A *trail!* It was all Morris could do to keep the smile from his face.

The lakeshore was cool; the water seemed to draw the heat from the morning air and hold it in the wreaths of mists that drifted across its surface. The far side of the lake was visible, but only as a distant blur of grey and brown smears. Was that a rocky shore? Foliage? Morris couldn't be sure.

This shore was a stretch of mud dotted with large and small grey rocks, some slick with lichen or moss and others bare, like ancient teeth lost in brown gums, and it was a treasure trove of evidence. The mud held fresh prints, which allowed Morris to judge that the thing was even bigger than they had first thought. All around the prints were long streaks and scars in the thick, damp ground. Close by was a stain that might have just been a darker strain of earth showing through, although Morris doubted it; he would take a sample and test it when he had the chance. Better yet, there was a pile of fresh shit near where the hat was found, a conical mass with the consistency of newly dug clay. Morris detailed Bailey to take samples, wincing as the man dug his hand deep into the scat with a look on his face not unlike glee. It stank, its tang sharp and acrid, and its colour was a vile chalky green.

They tried to follow the prints, tracking them back and forward from the lakeside in both directions. However, the trails became entangled with other animal tracks or simply faded away to nothing. They tried following some of the paths, branching off at various places where the tracks had doubled back on themselves and then gone a different way, but these also led to nothing. One of them took the party back towards the camp, ending in a confusion of overlapping and smudged prints just below the treeline. Standing in the patch of churned earth, Morris looked through the trees and saw the camp; most of the indentations, he noticed, faced the mass of tents not two or three hundred yards distant. He wondered if it was the smell of the cooking that had attracted it or the noise. He would be sure to tell everyone to keep the odours and their conversation to a minimum.

In the end, they set their trap and bait near the lakeshore; wrapped in foliage and packed full of fresh meat, the metal cage was hard to see but, hopefully, easy to smell. Even Morris, who knew it was there, could hardly make it out. Perched in a hastily constructed hide, Morris felt the excitement build in him. After all the planning, after all the false starts and failures, after the last nine days of travel and sites that turned out wrong, and inhospitable terrain, always searching and never finding, they were finally there. *Finally!* It was even worth putting up with Bailey's chirpiness, his whispered conversations and apparent stream-of-conscious-ness chatter of ideas and suggestions about the research they could do once they caught the creature. His noise filled the hide like smoke but Morris didn't try to shut him up; he knew from bitter experience that the man would continue until he fell asleep. All he could hope for was that his voice wouldn't escape the hide and scare the creature off.

The atmosphere changed.

Around them, silence had fallen, the silence of anticipation and of things hiding, observing. Morris knew it was unscientific, but he was sure he could sense the tension in the other hides, from the men with darts and nets and cameras and radios. Morris' breathing shortened and tightened. He leaned forward, pushing against the hide's wall and tried to peer further out through the observation slot. Even Bailey quietened. Nothing moved, nothing shrieked or roared or called.

Somewhere up the slope, the trees shivered although there

was no breeze to move them. The shiver approached, branches dancing lightly back and forth. He caught a whiff of something, acrid and heavy, and then a large shadow slipped across his vision, moving between the trunks like a patch of liquid blackness, approaching them fast.

Morris tensed; his time had arrived. Something was coming.

F Bomb

THE FIRST TIME it happened was on a Sunday afternoon, on a children's television channel.

The presenter, young but still with several years of live television experience behind her, was delivering a link between two programmes when, in the middle of her monologue, in which she was also providing the voice of the cuddly bear that was her companion that day, she swore. It was not because something had gone wrong unexpectedly, nor was it in response to surprise or pain; it was a simple, unthinking use of a single profane word three times in under a minute, twice as an adverb and once as a noun.

As she said it for the third time, it was obvious that the presenter realised what she had done. Flustered, she immediately apologised and, clearly upset and trying not to cry, turned to look at someone offscreen. Her apology was repeated as part of a formal statement released by the channel later the same day. It was read out between two programmes by the station's controller, and then repeated every hour as well as being released in as a press release. In the statement, the presenter apologised unreservedly and claimed that she

11

"had no idea why she said those things" and that she had "never made such a terrible mistake before". The channel suspended her without pay for four weeks, but the damage was done and the media lit upon the subject as their latest *bête noire*.

Over the next week, a number of articles appeared in both the tabloid and broadsheet publications discussing the encroachment of "inappropriate language" into daily life and the general lessening of linguistic standards across the country, with one or two television and radio debate shows also covering the subject. Most referenced the infamous Kenneth Tynan incident as well as other notable live *faux pas,* bracketing these verbal slips and tics under the cover-all term "F Bomb".

This phrase was first used as an article title by one of the tabloids in reference to the word that the presenter had used, and was soon picked up by the other broadcasters as a useful shorthand for swearing live on television. The furore over the incident fuelled a broader debate about standards in the media and in wider society, and all the major political parties used what happened to attack each other, criticising education provision and funding, mechanisms for control of the media and in one case talking about the less specific but more damaging notion of "poor moral standards and stewardship". Comedians used the situation as the basis for skits, both political and scatological, although most received poor reviews. After almost two weeks, the incident was beginning to fade from the public consciousness and the media had found other things to cover; overseas wars continued and there were new crimes occurring on their doorstep to report.

And then the newsreader on one of the major news channels used the word during an early evening bulletin.

The reaction was swift and loud, with revised versions of earlier articles appearing in most of the print media. Typical headlines included the *Sun*'s IT'S THE EFFING NEWS!, the *Daily Mirror*'s LOOKING BAD FOR NEWSREADER!, and *The Guardian*'s DEBATE ABOUT UNACCEPTABLE LANGUAGE REACHES PRIMETIME PROGRAMMING. The newsreader, like the children's presenter, immediately released a statement of apology and was suspended without pay but, unlike the previous incident, this outcry did not have a chance to fade when the next F Bomb occurred.

Six days after the newsreader's slip, the first nine minutes of a live football broadcast included thirty-eight uses of the word, spoken by both commentators (one a seasoned television veteran and the other a relatively new football pundit recently retired from playing the game). The two men were removed from the broadcast from the tenth minute on, and both later apologised, but by then it was too late. The issue was lodged solidly into public awareness, fixed there by opinion pieces and *vox pop* items discussing the use of the word, and the tabloid media demanding action on the "increasing use of foul and degrading language in everyday life". The government responded by setting up a taskforce to look at the situation.

The taskforce's initial investigations took four weeks, during which time the word was heard increasingly on pre-watershed live television and radio. In addition, it started to appear in other environments—MPs used it during commons debates without apparently realising it, it was heard during tannoy announcements in most of the major airports and train stations, several clergy were reported for using it during sermons and one for its use during a baptism ceremony, and at least one hospital consultant was suspended pending an investigation of her use of it during a routine consultation. By the time the taskforce chairman made his interim report, people reported hearing the word at least once or twice a day from sources that they would have not previously expected to use it.

The task force analysed a range of data from as many sources as they could bring in during the short time available to them, and its findings painted a grimmer picture than anyone expected. The use of the word in what it called "less sensitive and more tolerant arenas" (for example, post-watershed television or live broadcast performances) had increased by just over one hundred percent in the previous six months, but its use pre-watershed had increased nearly one thousand percent. Concurrent to this, schools reported a trebling of children referred to child mental health services or excluded from school for sustained and inappropriate use of the word. During the same period, NHS and social service departments received increased complaints made against their staff for the use of the word or its variations, as did those businesses who responded to the taskforce's requests for information and were able to provide figures. Teachers, nurses, doctors, social workers, care assistants and a number of other professional bodies questioned by the task force all reported that the use of the word by members of the public had jumped noticeably in the previous months; the only areas in which its use seemed to have not changed was in the print media.

The task force (dubbed *Britain's FBI: F Bomb Investigators* by one newspaper) came to expected conclusions—that the responsibility lay with everyone to try to curb the word's use, and with the media particularly to prevent its occurrence in live broadcasts at any time. It lamented the declining social standards that led to the word being more acceptable, recommended harsher punishments for transgressors, and suggested the adoption of voluntary 'language codes' for institutions such as schools, hospitals, offices, bars, nightclubs, and public transport. Its ultimate aim, said the chairman, was to stimulate debate and to facilitate "a return to the values of a time when that word was rightly shocking and its use both less frequent and more considered". During the presentation of the task force's findings, the chairman deviated from his prepared speech, using the word seven times.

Later, Mulgrew decided that he had probably come into contact with the F Bomb about a week earlier than its first public appearance. Of course, at the time, he didn't see it for what it was; it was simply an incident, and it came before him as part of his routine duties. The position of Head of Department, shared between the three senior staff members, was newly his and one of the first jobs of his twelve-month tenure was to chair a complaint panel.

"She swore at me!" said Pumphrey, a second-year student. "I asked her if I could get a copy of the handouts I'd missed because I was ill, and she told me to...well...to...you know...off."

"Did you?" Mulgrew asked Doyle, the lecturer. Pumphrey had gone red and wouldn't say the offending word. Mulgrew wanted to smile at the boy's innocence, but didn't.

"Yes," said Doyle simply. "It wasn't intentional, and I don't normally swear. I don't know why it slipped out, but it did. I apologised straight away, and I've apologised since." Pumphrey nodded in agreement.

"And have you got the handouts now?"

"Yes, but when she gave them me, Miss Doyle swore again!" the student replied miserably. Mulgrew looked questioningly at Doyle. She nodded and said "True".

After the panel had finished, Mulgrew spoke with Doyle; he liked her and knew she was an easygoing lecturer, and her behaviour towards Pumphrey was out of character. Although he had had little choice to but to formally reprimand her, he wanted to know if there was anything bothering her that she couldn't or wouldn't say during the meeting. They talked as they walked across the campus.

"There's nothing wrong," Doyle assured him as they arrived at the department corridor. "I meant what I said. I don't dislike the kid, I wasn't having a bad day, but when he asked me a question, I answered and those words just kind of slipped out. I'll try to make sure it doesn't happen again." She looked tired, Mulgrew thought, as he watched her go into her office. He wondered if she knew that she'd been swearing whilst she spoke to him. No, not swearing, using one specific word repeatedly.

"It's a meme," said the woman from the philosophy department whose name he had not caught. Mulgrew hadn't thought about Doyle again until he saw the reports about the children's television presenter and then, less than a fortnight later, watched and listened as the newsreader used the same word. These things had struck him as odd, but nothing more, but now he was at a cross-faculty social and everyone seemed to be talking about it. Mulgrew was there only because his presence was expected and his absence would have been noted. He hated these things, hated the false bonhomie of them, hated the cheap wine the university provided but most of all, hated getting caught in corners with people he neither knew nor had anything in common with. The philosophy woman was a good example; she had discovered he was the head of the English Department and had immediately started talking to him about the F Bomb, thinking him interested when in truth, he wasn't.

"We're seeing the spread of a new cultural artefact," the woman carried on. "Passing from person to person, expanding and becoming the norm. It's what memes do, all those little pieces of information and sayings, it's how they spread. Like a virus. It's a meme." She looked expectantly at Mulgrew, waiting for his response, but he honestly wasn't sure what was expected of him. Agreement? He had no idea if the woman was right or not, and wasn't sure what to say, but then someone else answered for him and saved him the trouble.

"Of course it's not a meme."

The speaker was a little, pale man who stepped around the woman and inserted himself into the conversation space. He grinned at Mulgrew, his watery eyes twinkling, and turned to the woman. "It's mimicking the way a meme spreads, to be sure, but it's not a new cultural artefact. The word that everyone's using is an old one, centuries old actually. It isn't newly arrived or experiencing a shift in status or meaning, so it's not a meme."

"Well, what is it then? And who are you?" asked the woman. *The woman's name was Porter*, Mulgrew suddenly remembered. Porter, newly arrived in the philosophy department, specialising (she had proudly told him) in ontological thought in the twenty-first century.

"Goldberg," replied the man. "I'm in psychology, researching language acquisition and usage. I thought about the meme idea for a while as well, you know, but it's not. If anything, it's closer in analogy to what you mentioned before that."

Porter looked puzzled. Goldberg, the grin never leaving his face, said, "That it's a virus."

The woman's mouth fell open and even Mulgrew blinked at this. "A virus?"

"Bear with me," said Goldberg. "We all have filters, we use them all the time, even though we don't know it. We don't swear, we don't insult people even if we feel we might want to. It's one of the things that enable us to function as a social animal. You see the result of these filters breaking down in conditions like Tourette's Syndrome, where individuals can't help what comes out of their mouths, and are frequently ostracised as a result. Here it's as though one incredibly specific filter, dealing with that word alone, is failing, which is very odd. Of course, we might be tempted to interpret it as a meme, or as a sudden and unexpected social shift. In sociological terms, of course, it's unusual but not unheard of and it could be, I suppose, an attitude alteration forced by simple over-exposure to the word. In those circumstances, you'd see a change in social constructs which removes the word's power to shock and offend. If that's the case, it's nothing more than a social adjustment and we'll get used to it."

"But?" asked Mulgrew, hearing the unspoken word in the cadence of Goldberg's voice.

"But that's not right in this case, not really, is it? Go and watch the film of the children's TV presenter, or the newsreader, really *watch* it. They weren't using the word deliberately, to be provocative or to push some notional boundary, and they weren't using it because it's normal to them; it's not a meme because this isn't a new word, or a new configuration of the word that they're using, and know that they're using. No, they were genuinely surprised by what was coming out of their mouths, and they didn't choose what they said. It's a mystery, and as such it's as easy to argue that they've picked up a virus, an incredibly contagious infection that attacks one specific linguistic filter but has no other visible symptoms. It simply lets that word out into everyday speech as unconsciously as breathing."

"Nonsense," said Porter. "People's brains can be affected

by illness, yes, but when we're ill, pressured, or in the grip of mind-altering drugs like alcohol we don't just increase the use of one word, we use all of those normally forbidden words to a greater extent."

"I agree," said Goldberg. "This isn't a virus any more than it's a meme."

"So what is it?" asked Porter, and the cheap wine had put an edge of aggression into her voice. Mulgrew unobtrusively moved away from her, leaving Goldberg to fend for himself. The last thing he heard the man say was, "I don't know, but it should be interesting finding out, shouldn't it?" before the other sounds of the party overwhelmed them and Mulgrew was free.

Meme or virus, Mulgrew's interest was piqued and he began to watch more television and listen to people around him more closely. It was true, he realised, people were using the word more often, and from the perspective of someone who studied and loved language it was both fascinating and horrifying. For years, the word had lurked around the edges of, if not respectability then certainly some form of acceptance, but now it was *everywhere*. People were driven to use it, he saw, could not stop once they had started, were compelled in some way by something that wouldn't let them be, keep pushing at them. He heard people say the word, start at what they had just said, apologise and say it again in their apology. When Mulgrew watched them speak, he saw frustration, anger, shame, and helplessness; he heard a word emerging like an unwanted parasite leaving its host. He heard it in coffee shops, in supermarkets, on the street, used as a verb and adverb, as noun and an adjective, until eventually it seemed, to Mulgrew's ears, to almost lose its meaning and become a kind of grim, abrasive punctuation within speech rather than part of the speech itself.

"I had another idea," said Goldberg, "that I've also dismissed."

They were sitting in one of the campus coffee shops, crowds bustling and swearing around them. Mulgrew had bumped into Goldberg earlier that morning, and his growing interest in the F Bomb had led him to ask the man if he had made any progress on discovering its cause.

"I wondered for a while if it wasn't some kind of social engineering experiment, but that's almost certainly not it," said Goldberg. "For it to have been that, what you'd need is a coordinated use of the word by willing participants, and most people don't seem to want to use it, do they?"

"No," agreed Mulgrew.

"Besides, if it was social engineering, the best that the engineers could hope for is that people, exposed to the word, make a slip and use the word once or twice so that eventually, as a society, we'd see a subsequent lessening of the word's shock value and an increase in what we might call its 'normal' use." Goldberg stopped for a moment, his eyes focussing on something in a place that Mulgrew couldn't see.

"I wondered instead if it wasn't some kind of singularity, some kind of event horizon, that using the word more and more was like the compacting of time around a black hole," continued Goldberg quietly, drinking more of his coffee. "I thought that perhaps we were heading to some literal cultural F Bomb moment, after which every word spoken would be that word, although I don't know what that would mean. But that's not right either, is it? People's usage of it doesn't increase incrementally, they just start using it but the amount of their new usage remains constant. We've had people come into the lab for us, we've analysed it so we know that's true."

Mulgrew waited. Goldberg was speaking almost to himself now, looking into his empty cup, his voice low. "People are talking less, we know that from the few experiments and analysis we've managed to do. They don't want to say the word, but they can't help it, so they simply reduce the amount they talk. You can tell which ones try to fight against using the word; they speak slowly, enunciate each word carefully. They look exhausted. Have you noticed a change in the conversations you've had with people recently?"

Mulgrew thought for a minute, and then nodded. "Yes. They only ever seem to be about the nuts and bolts of life and nothing more. People only ever seem to want to swap information in small pieces. It's like we're communicating at a reduced level."

"Precisely. Maybe we're looking at this wrong, maybe the question we should be concentrating on shouldn't be 'what is it?', but 'what's its purpose?'"

"Purpose?" asked Mulgrew. He had never thought of the F Bomb having a purpose before, he'd always assumed that it was something chaotic, purposeless. He finished his own coffee, seeing the reflection of his face in the dregs at the bottom of the cup as a trapped, encircled thing.

"There are no random events, not at a social or cultural level. The repetition of the word is part of a bigger, newly formed pattern, one in which language is changing, becoming something terse and utilitarian. We're losing the poetry of the everyday because no one will risk speaking in case that word emerges. Even people who haven't been caught by it yet speak less, have you noticed? It's as though they're frightened of speaking in case it happens." Mulgrew nodded, but did not reply.

That night, Mulgrew sat in his study and reread aloud some of his favourite poems, glorying in the richness and language, and the dip and sway of their rhythms. This was language unfettered, given the freedom of air and tongue and he bathed in it as it swooped around his room. He danced through Shakespeare's sonnets, touched upon Shelley and Peter Porter, trailed though Byron and Milligan, and the song lyrics of Leonard Cohen before sweeping back to Angelou and some of the emerging poets, Hadley, Baxter, and Ellis, before ending with Betjeman. He read several pieces aloud, and it was only when he reached the line, "And the vox humana swells" that he started to weep.

The next morning, when he arrived at the department, he greeted the secretary by swearing at her.

"I have another idea, if you're interested?"

The two of them were in the same coffee shop, now near-deserted. The only other person present was the waitress, who had taken their order without talking or looking at either of them. There were few people out in public these days; most stayed indoors now except for work or other vital appointments. The waitress, after putting their drinks on the table, retreated into the kitchen and a moment later a radio crackled into life, faint and indistinct like the voice of a ghost.

Goldberg hadn't grown any less pale since he and Mulgrew had last spoken but he had developed a slow, clench-jawed way of speaking that Mulgrew recognised from those around him and from looking at himself in the mirror—the man had been caught by the F Bomb and was fighting it. Dense pouches of bruised and tired flesh hung under his red-rimmed and bloodshot eyes and stubble gathered across his cheeks and chin. The previous night, after trying to read poetry out loud, and with their fractured and battered shadows had still hovering around him, Mulgrew had rung Goldberg. He did so not because he liked the man, but because he wanted to be with someone who might understand, who could talk about the F Bomb. Mulgrew swore when he spoke now, so that he avoided speaking whenever possible. Conversation felt like a skill, an *art*, he was losing, and he hated it. *Hated* it.

"We're evolving. You know that evolution moves in fits and starts rather than straight lines, that it relies on catastrophes to kick-start new developments or end failed ones? Like an asteroid kills the dinosaurs and gives the mammals supremacy, a landmass shifts open and closes migration routes, or provides or takes away food sources? Evolution uses these events as the impetus to move the species along until the next paradigm shift. That's all this is, a disaster leading to the next step forward."

Mulgrew tried to speak and the word slipped out, emerging from his open mouth like a snake. His lips curled back, clenched down, to stop it happening again and Goldberg, seeing him, waved his hand wearily.

"Don't talk, just think. What if the F Bomb is a step in an evolutionary process designed to change mankind?" Goldberg's own speech was slow, each word separated by a moment of thought, an inhalation and exhalation to trap the unwanted word and let the wanted one out. It was like listening to a machine communicate, grinding and precise and *wretched*.

"I think evolution is forcing us in a new direction, making it harder for us to care about each other, driving us away from our roots as social animals. We're becoming increasingly selfish, offensive, physically and emotionally aggressive, unconcerned about the feelings of others, focussed only on our own gratification. It's been happening for decades, and the F Bomb is simply another part of it. Evolution is forcing us to swear, to hate the language we use, to further alienate those around us, to stop communicating at anything but the basest levels. To become unlovable and unloved."

Goldberg placed his face in his hands and his next few words were so muffled that Mulgrew couldn't hear them. Eventually, Goldberg raised his head and looked across the table. There were tears in his eyes.

"This morning I tried to sing my favourite song and I couldn't. I either sing without thinking, in which case I use that word and the song is changed by its addition, buried under it, or I have to think about every word which slows it down, meaning it has no spontaneity, is without emotion or passion. I, *we*, are losing the ability to connect with art, and if art is removed from us, if the ability to talk about art is gone, then we become little more than animals."

Goldberg stopped, his jaw working against the word that must be roiling and shifting, inexorable, in his mouth. "Without art, without the ability to share our experiences, we become less able to relate to each other, less inclined to find common ground or to like each other. We'll lose the ability to value each other or be valued. We won't *care* any more. And the worst of it is, the F Bomb is a step, but it's not the last step. Just watch, it'll get worse from here. More unacceptable things will become normalised, there'll be more tension, more anger escaping, more violence until eventually, we'll have no filters left, not linguistic or emotional or physical."

"And then?" Mulgrew managed. His jaw ached from the effort of so solidly forming just two words, from ensuring that the words that came out were the words he wanted to utter. He felt a wave of helpless, ragged anger wash through him, burning like old, sour bile.

"At a guess? We'll be completely detached from each other, which I suppose is the point. Together, we're destructive, parasitical, planetary abusers, but alone we're nothing. We're vulnerable. I suspect the aim is to reduce us, make us smaller. Make us *less*. And then? Anarchy, chaos, until eventually we get replaced, lose our position of primacy on top of the evolutionary pile. And there's nothing we can do about it."

Goldberg stood. His jaw was clenched, veins writhing under the skin like cables. The effort of speaking for so long without swearing was written across his forehead in sweat strings and in the dull glint of his eyes. His hands were closed into fists and Mulgrew wondered if this was the next stage, the emergence of violence as a way of releasing the fear and tension that writhed inside people. He felt tiny and helpless and angry and he clenched his own fists in case he needed to retaliate. Goldberg was right—he was being lessened, and the urge was in him to scream and shout about it, to punch and kick, to strike out and draw blood, to communicate in blows and aggression, to release his fury any way he could, and to mark the world in bruises and blows.

No, it was too big a jump; whatever happened next would be logical, so that the majority of people wouldn't notice it as part of a chain, not until it was too late. Evolution used catastrophes, true, but the movements between these catastrophes were tiny, infinitesimal increments, gathering pace and weight without being seen until it was too late and their massed momentum was irresistible and their accumulated profile unrecognisable, vast. The next stage wouldn't be violence, but something that built on the F Bomb to further offend and abrade and weaken. Violence would come later.

As Goldberg turned and walked away, the waitress came out from the kitchen. Before the door swung shut behind her, Mulgrew heard a news report on the distant radio. Somehow, he wasn't surprised when he heard the phrase *The C Bomb*.

THE HOTEL GUEST

THE ELEVATOR DOORS opened and Parnell was out before he realised that the floor he had entered was wrong.

Not the wrong floor, although Lord knows he had done that before, but *wrong*. He should have walked out into the hotel's main bar, found it full of weary conventioneers making their way to breakfast in the dining room. They had been here not five minutes ago when he had popped back to his room to get his phone; hungover, subdued, in some cases still drunk, clutching at advertisements and programmes, but nonetheless *there*. And now there was no one.

Parnell heard the elevator doors *clunk* behind him and turned to find them shut. Streaks of rust bled away from the join between the doors, the smears orange-brown in the dull light. Rust? The elevator doors hadn't been rusty before. Dirty and old, yes; he had complained about them and about the poor quality of the fittings in his room yesterday without success, but not rusty. The streaks glittered, seemingly drawing light in but letting nothing out. Besides, there wasn't just rust, there was something like black, oily moss creeping

27

along the lower edges of the doors, glistening sickly. Parnell went to push the call button to re-open the doors, but stopped. More of the moss was furred thickly around the raised nubbin, burying itself into the join between it and the surrounding plate. It looked wet and unhealthy and he did not want to touch it.

Looking around, he saw that the moss was growing all over the room; great sweeps of it clung to the joins between the floor and the walls as though it were seeping in from outside, and more crept up the front of the bar itself. The brass foot-rail was almost lost beneath its black touch and its twin, lining the upper edge of the bar, was rapidly being smothered beneath another dark slick. Even those areas that the moss had not covered looked lustreless and empty; the metal pumps' curved surfaces showing only the dimmest of reflections. Behind the bar, the shelves and optics were empty. How could they be empty? Last night there had been bottle after bottle there, serried ranks like glass soldiers standing or hanging, all bleeding out for the massed throng that filled the public space with sweat and noise, and the odour of alcohol and excitement. Parnell had gone to bed relatively early, but surely there was no way his fellow attendees could have drunk the bar empty, could they? No. He might have dismissed them the night before as fools, as hopeless drinkers, but this had been a well-stocked bar. It would not have run dry. A heavy coat of something that looked damp and filthy lay across the empty shelves and covered the mirrored rear walls like a cataract. Parnell, a feeling of uncomfortable, loose panic building in his belly, went to the dining area.

The serving trays, set into a broad table top under a clear Perspex hood, and normally swimming in sausages, bacon, eggs, mushrooms, and other breakfast fixings, were full of grease. It was old and solid, with ripples of something almost black running through its yellow heart in frozen twists. In places, grease had spilled out and down onto the floor where the moss nibbled at its edges. Further into the room, tables were scattered across the floor with chairs heaped around them like piles of autumn leaves. A dank smell of corrupted meat and things left in dark corners to rot laced the air. There was less black moss in here but more rust streaks, falling away from the wall lamps and spreading lazily from the ceiling lights. They stained the pale cream paint a colour that looked, in the dim light, like dried blood. Perhaps it *was* dried blood, thought Parnell, and then dismissed the idea angrily. Walls did not bleed.

But people, it seemed, vanished.

Actually, Parnell was less bothered by the lack of people than he was by the sudden changes in the hotel itself. He had stayed in enough places like this over the years that he could well believe he had found one of those odd, quiet lacunae between the flow of people and staff, a moment in the life of the building between the beats of its vast heart when things were caught, motionless. No, it was the other things. The moss, and the rust that looked like blood for a start, but it was more than that, much more. There were wide, dirty streaks running along the carpet and back out into the bar, and the carpet was buckled and swollen where it met the skirting. It looked as though the room was drying after being soaked in dank water, and the carpet itself felt tacky and clinging when he knelt and touched it. His fingertips came away with light grey circles of damp dirt on them. He brushed it off on his trousers, where it left pale marks. The hotel was overpriced, dirty and run down, yes, but this was ridiculous.

His mobile phone didn't work. Well, it did, but not properly—he had a dial tone but no matter how hard or desperately he punched at the keys, nothing happened and the phone's display obstinately refused to show anything other than his wallpaper, a picture of him and Judy before things went sour. Even the picture seemed wrong somehow, as though it had distorted in subtle, almost unknowable ways. Had he always looked so small in the picture? Had Judy always been so *grey*? He didn't think so. The signal strength indicator was at zero.

Back in the bar, Parnell tried shouting. "Hello?" he called, hesitant at first and then louder. "Hello? *Hello*!" and then louder and more hysterical, and all the anxiety came roaring out of him in screams. He doubled over from the effort of shrieking, losing the words in his outburst and falling back on incoherent howls of noise designed solely to bring someone running to him. *Someone will pay for this nonsense*, he was thinking as he screamed, *someone will be sorry for this crap*.

No one came.

He had no idea how long he screamed for; in the end he stopped because no one responded and because his throat was roaring fire. He coughed miserably, bending and spitting onto the carpet, where his saliva sank into the thin fibres. Out here, he saw more of the stains across the floor. Some looked almost like trails, others as though something had been dragged, leaking, to somewhere else in the building. By the lifts, one of them disappeared under the edge of the black moss, which looked like it had grown in the few minutes he had been in the dining room. That was stupidity, of course, nothing grew that fast. He looked around the bar again, trying to ignore the fact that the pictures lining the walls looked different from the uninspiring prints that had been up yesterday. The images were almost the same but where yesterday the frames had held bland photographs of country houses, now the houses looked warped, their open faces turned to sneers. He decided that he could not stay here.

Screaming seemed to have taken his panic away for now, so Parnell came up with a plan—to go to the foyer to see if there was an explanation for what was happening and, if not, out of the hotel and onto the streets of Nottingham. *Surely I'll find someone,* he told himself as he went to the wide stairs. *Surely there's someone around besides me.* Then he stopped because he saw the graffiti.

It was scrawled on the wall at the turn of the stairs in letters that were large and dark and written in liquid that had dried and flaked in patches, leaving pale ghosts of the letters behind.

SHHHHHHHHHH

The last letter fell away, as though whoever had written it had been leaning out too far, or had fallen as they wrote. Beneath was a smaller phrase that Parnell had to get closer to read: *It can hear.*

It can hear? Parnell thought. *What can? Hear what? What is this crap?* He went down the stairs at an almost-run, feeling the bubbles of panic play across his tongue and kiss at his teeth as he went, knowing he had to keep moving or else he might stop, start screaming and not stop until he tore himself inside out. That was what Judy would expect of him after all; to fall apart, to lose his temper, lose control, to *be useless,* to *complain.*

The foyer was as deserted as the bar. A neat pile of newspapers stood on the reception desk but when Parnell tried to pick one up to read the date or headlines, it disintegrated into damp grey pulp. Behind the desk, the receptionist's chair glistened with moss that grew wetly over the seat and up the chair back. The computer screen was dark and its keyboard crusted with something that had dried to a thick, glutinous yellow. It was the brightest colour Parnell had seen since emerging from the lift. Beside the computer was a box of printouts, bills and checking-in information, but these too fell apart when he leaned over and tried to pull them from the box. The smell in the foyer was fainter than in the kitchen but still noticeable. The walls were damp, glistening with moisture.

"Hello!" Parnell called again, no longer expecting a response but hoping for one anyway. Echoes of his voice came back to him in descending ripples. Yesterday, the floor of the foyer had been varnished wood, clean and shining. Now, it was dull, streaked with something flaked away into white drifts like peeled skin when he kicked at them. As they broke apart, the streaks released another smell, fetid and sharp. It reminded Parnell of bad breath made worse and he stepped away to escape it. The glass exit doors beckoned.

They would not open. He shook them hard and although they gave slightly, they would not swing fully in or out. He shook them again, becoming angry as he did so, and started shouting, screaming obscenities as he kicked the doors. The glass did not break. Parnell's spittle decorated the upper pane, flecking across the grimy surface in tiny, seed-like blobs. Eventually, he took one of the foyer chairs and threw it at the doors, a furious howl escaping his lips as he did so. It smacked dully against the panes and fell back to the floor at his feet, one of its legs buckled. The glass was unmarked, the doors unharmed.

He was trapped.

Parnell flattened himself against the glass, shouting. His breath fogged the pane, a misted patch raising itself in front of his eyes and blocking his view for a moment. The glass smelled unwashed, was greasy against his splayed palms and cheek. Outside, the road sloped away from the hotel's entrance, deserted and grey and not right; it caught him, this *not-rightness* and he stopped shouting, peering at the world beyond the doors. It looked flat, as though it were a giant painting rather than a real thing, not genuine or even a faked attempt at genuine but simply a picture of something designed as a background and not for use.

"I will not panic," he said out loud, trying to ignore the tremble in his voice. "I will not become a *pointless drama queen.*" Judy's phrase, thrown at him in anger during their last argument. *I will not be that person,* he thought. *I will not.*

If he could not escape from the front, he needed to look for another exit, or for anything that might help explain what was happening. He would be logical, be sensible. He would be rational, even in the face of the irrational. Methodically, he climbed the stairs and looked into every corridor. The first and second were deserted and appeared mostly how they ought to look—the carpets were unstained, the walls untouched by moss or rust, the room doors shut and locked. He tried to open several, but they remained solidly closed. The third floor showed some signs of decay and the air was warmer, humid, and dank. The walls sweated, droplets of moisture gathering in the embossed patterns of the wallpaper and trickling down to the carpet. The ceiling was covered in ringed stains, flowering from black centres to ruby edges in irregular ovals and circles. He did not try to open any of the doors on the third corridor; the handles looked tarnished and grey and he did not like the way the carpet felt under his feet when he walked towards the nearest door. It was springy and uneven, as though he was moving across damp and rotten wood. On the fourth floor, the heavy door separating the stairwell from the bedrooms was hanging open, its frame swollen and warped. The corridor beyond it was rimed in growths that started on the floor and slithered up the walls, bulging and fungal and fetid. He did not enter, merely looking in from the doorway and breathing deeply. The air was hazy with spores, and he could taste them as he breathed, feel them brush against his tongue and tickle at his throat. He spat, but their taste did not go away. *I will not panic*, he repeated to himself. *I will not.*

The fifth floor, where Parnell's room was located, was in an even worse state. Flanks of grime lined walls that were buckled and swollen and which bulged out at odd, bloated angles into the corridor. The floor was uneven, like the deck of a ship that, although motionless, was nonetheless swaying to some rhythm that only it knew. When he pushed his hands tentatively against the wall, he felt the plaster give under his fingertips, its paper covering tearing wetly as his fingers disappeared into a soggy mess of dust and liquid. His fingers emerged coated with slimy, pale residue and brought with them a vile smell, rich and corrupt. He choked on it, its rancid touch causing his throat to clench shut and bile to swirl amongst the panic he felt scratching at him. Backing away, he bumped into an occasional table which fell; it tilted with a noise like undercooked flesh coming away from the bone. Where its feet had been, the carpet had torn away. Wisps of the fibres clung to the table legs, hanging loosely down.

Suddenly furious, Parnell kicked out at the table. His foot lashed against it and it disintegrated into sodden strands, strings of wood spattering across the wall and his toecap. There were no jagged, dried wood splinters here, only fibres of pale flesh that twisted and clung like seaweed. He kicked again, anger forcing more sounds from his bruised throat. Again and again he kicked, his feet tearing at the table, faster and faster until there was little left except for a pile of moist, shredded crap. Even then, he stamped, flattening it into a pale bloom against the dark, uneven floor.

Spent, Parnell slumped, his fury replaced by shame. *What's that achieved?* he thought. *Really? What?* He remembered Judy in that last argument, her face red and swelling, her eyes narrowed to feline slits. "It's always the same, you can't keep your temper. You say you will, but you don't. It always happens, the slightest thing and you're off, and do you know what? It's always about *you*, your feelings, your inconvenience, never anyone else." Parnell had wanted to reply, to deny, but could not. The mark on Judy's cheek spoke its own language, was a proof he could not hope to deny, and he knew it and hated it. Could not change it.

There was more graffiti in the stairwell, and it had not been there when he passed earlier, he was sure of it. It was written in the condensation that trickled down the walls, the strokes a finger's width set of tracks through the moisture.

IT WILL NOTICE YOU

"Who the fuck is there?" called Parnell, not liking the way his voice cracked and wheezed through his throat. "What the fuck is this?" No one replied. The echoes of his voice came back to him in reducing morsels until they, too, were gone. Parnell waited, hoping for the scatter of feet or the distant notice of someone talking, moving, breathing. Anything.

Nothing.

Parnell went further up the stairs. Instead of looking into each corridor, he continued to the very top of the hotel, to the thirteenth floor. He was not superstitious, but the irony of it was grand, just *grand*. He was in a hotel that was rotting away, deserted, not the hotel he had woken up in that morning, and he had ended up on the thirteenth floor. *Brilliant*, he thought bitterly. *Fucking brilliant.* The smell was lighter on the uppermost floor, less *there*, as though it were simply a drifting odour from somewhere else rather than from something belonging to the floor itself. Parnell tried to force himself to relax, slumping against the window.

From here, he could see the whole town. Or rather, he couldn't; the impressions gained looking through the hotel's front doors were reinforced. He was looking not at a view, so much as a picture of a view; something painted or printed on the other side of the glass. It was flat, lifeless. Nothing moved in the grey streets, no birds flew in the sky, no shops were open. And yet, there must be life somewhere. Someone was in the hotel, even if they were avoiding him, leaving him cryptic messages on the walls instead of talking to him.

"It's always about you, isn't it?" asked Judy, unbidden, in his mind. "It's never about anyone else, is it? Same old selfish man, unable to think that other people might do things that aren't about you. How do you know they're hiding from you? They could be hiding from something else."

Something else?

What?

Parnell tried to open the window, but could not. He had the half-formed notion of breaking the glass, and calling for help, or climbing down the outside of the building, but that also proved impossible. He broke two chairs against its unforgiving solidity and then bruised his knuckles when he punched at it, his fury and fear making him lose control again for the briefest of moments before he pulled himself back, became calm once more. It was only a few minutes after that that he found tears trickling down his face.

In the end, he paced most of the day away, wandering corridor after corridor with no real plan or destination in mind. He tried windows and doors randomly, but none of the windows and few of the doors opened, leaving him instead to navigate around hallways and stairwells that were growing warmer as the hours passed, their corners and ceilings stained and furred with dank growths and lifeless, weeping droplets of water.

He found the cleaner's closet on the eighth floor.

Parnell saw from a distance that something was happening behind the closed closet door. A pool of viscous yellow liquid was seeping out from under the door, staining the carpet amber. The air smelled of something he could not properly identify. It was dense, peaty and sour and fleshy all at once and the closer he got to the door, the stronger the smell became. It was hotter near the door, and when he stood in front of it (avoiding the sticky pool), Parnell could *feel* the heat wafting off the door in sick waves. Trembling, he pulled at the door which, to his surprise, opened. He didn't really want to see into the room, but he *had* to. He wanted an explanation for this, a reason, a solution. A fucking apology.

At first, he saw nothing. Shelves lined the walls and fell away into the darkness at the room's rear; pale wood and dull metal losing itself in shadow. Bottles and tubs lined the shelves and an old mop bucket brushed the shadow line, its dented carapace like a tortoise's shell. Parnell opened the door wider, letting light fall into the room's depths. He saw the way the wall bulged and the way it had twisted into fungal growths, saw the way growths licked out and swallowed the shelves and were creeping across the carpet and shelves, saw the streaks of lurid yellow liquid and glinting black skeins that slithered through the bulge, smelled the ripe odour of things that grow in lightless places. He choked, stepped back hoping to see no more.

Saw that twisted shape that lay at the heart of the growths.

It might, once, have been a person. Although it was entirely covered, he saw in the uneven bulge the impression of arms, a head, and legs bunched up tight into a foetal ball.

Was that a hand, clawed fingers almost poking through the moss? And an elbow pushing out against the leathery skin of the fungus, a foot pressing against the side of the ballooning wall? The way the yellow liquid pooled there, *there* and *there* created shapes of the indentations, eyes and an open, screaming mouth; a face? Was there a person in there? Someone lost in the black moss and weeping bile and walls that seemed to have swelled like inflating cheeks?

No. *No.*

Nonsense. It could not be. Parnell stepped away from the door and kicked it shut, enjoying the way it shivered as it slammed into the frame and the way his toecap left a crescent scar in the dark varnish. "No," he said aloud, and "No" again, louder. Firmer. He kicked out at the door again, liked the way the wood pulped under his foot without resistance and came away in wet strings that sucked at his shoes and trouser cuffs. Liked its weakness, liked that he could damage it with little effort. Another kick; another dent and wood peeling away in long, damaged fingers, and then "No," one last time, followed by a snarled "Fuck you!" for good measure, and a final kick.

Parnell's foot went all the way through the door with a flatulent ripping sound and suddenly he was panicking. What if the black moss caught his foot? What if that yellow ichor dripped against him, or the walls swelled to grip him like the poor bastard in there? He pulled his foot back, yanking it hard against wood that suddenly seemed to have a pincer's grip. "Let go!" he shouted, yanking again, and then he was free and falling.

He fell back against the wall opposite the door and for an awful moment he wasn't sure it would hold. It sagged, giving behind him, cocooning him in wallpaper and plaster that was soft and warm and oddly fleshy. He struggled, waving his arms like a swimmer thrashing in open water and managed to lurch forward, forcing gravity to release him from the wall's miserably tender hold. He dropped to his knees, looking around; there was a dent in the wall where he had struck it, a distorted oval that even now was filling with trickles of yellowing water that gathered at the edges of the dip and dribbled into it, pooling at its lowest point. The liquid looked thick, too thick to be just water and Parnell rose and backed away down the corridor as quickly as he could. It was only as he turned to enter the stairwell that he saw the graffiti.

IT CAN FEEL YOU

And below it, smaller: *You are being noticed.*

This time, Parnell didn't even call out when he read the message, too tired and too bewildered to care who was writing them and choosing to remain hidden. *Fine, let them hide. Fuck them.* He'd figure this out for himself, work out what was going on and find a way out for himself. He didn't need anyone—not the mysterious message-writer, not the silly sods from the convention, not Judy. Certainly not Judy, with her "Oh, don't be such an irritant" and "I'll never forgive you" comments and her swollen face that he had once found attractive. If he was an irritant, it had only been because she had driven him to it with her constant nagging and lazy assumptions, conclusions, and her look of condescending understanding. *Fuck all of them!* Parnell would find his own solution.

Eventually, because he did not know what else to do, Parnell headed back to his room. He had spent what little remained of the day traipsing all around the hotel, but had found no clues as to what was happening, and no exits. Every window he tried to open or break, every external door he tried to open remained stubbornly closed. Unlike the internal doors and walls, they did not break or splinter easily, did not give in to him no matter how frantic he became. He had returned to the kitchen at one point, wondering about food and drink, but the smell had quickly put him off; it smelled like sickness and shit and old milk, rich and raw and soured. The weight of the odour hit his stomach and curled his hunger back like peeling paint. Even the sealed bottles of water were off somehow, the liquid inside seemed to slosh too heavily, was murky behind the grimy plastic, and thicker than water ought to be. He left it. He wanted to cry, but would not let himself. Instead, clutching at what little self-control he had left he returned to the fifth floor. He had avoided it all day, superstitiously hoping that if he did not see it, then nothing would be wrong with it.

It was worse than he could have imagined.

The walls had swollen, were bulging, taking away the hallway's angularity and making it organic, tube-like. The walls wept condensation and the floor beneath the carpet gave beneath his feet, not buckling so much as *deflating* under him, as though he were walking on puffy, infected flesh rather than wood and metal and fabric. Everything had darkened, flushing to angry reds and purples and not the dull beiges and creams that he had left this morning. Moss and growths slithered around the doorways and across the floor, and more rust streaks dripped above him; the liquid that fell from them tinged pink and yellow. His own door was neither better nor worse than the others; the wood was wet, rippled and warped, but his card key still fitted into the slot and there was an answering blink of green LED that made him close his eyes in mute thanks. Pushing gingerly at the door, he looked in on his room.

Only it wasn't his room, not really; it was like a poor reflection of the place he had left that morning, when the worst thing that he expected to see was the people from the convention and the worst he expected to feel was that slow, helpless burn of anger at Judy rather than this gibbering, clawing helplessness and fear. This morning, his room had been shabbily furnished and poorly cleaned, small and devoid of anything approaching a personality, but it had at least been *his*, even if only for a short time. This room was dark and smelled heavily of damp. The bed was furred with spores that looked like elongated dust and the tiny dressing table was already sagging, its legs bowing and moist. Not his, but *nearly* his; the bedclothes were rumpled in a way he recognised, the towels just visible on the bathroom floor were piled where he had left them, and the shape against the far wall might be his bag. He hesitated, wondering what to do, and then realised that he had nowhere else to be, nowhere to go. He went in.

Shutting the door helped. It didn't fit properly back into the frame, but he pushed it and forced it closed. Impressions of his hands were visible for a few moments in the wood before they filled out, and Parnell could have sworn that the indentations were paler than the rest of the wood, darkening only as the door's flesh swelled into the holes. Experimentally, he pushed against the door again, pulling away to see a deep dent that was definitely paler than the rest of the wood. As he watched, it flushed darker and bubbled, filling out. Retreating from it, Parnell felt the weeping start and bit down on it; *no*. Judy had told him that he should be in touch with his emotions, be more honest with himself and others, but look where that had got him. He had let the anger come, let the fury show through fully that one time, and she had left him because of it. It had been her fault, really, goading him about his procrastination, his temper, his uncaring attitude, his selfishness, his inability to talk to her, and in the end, his hand had acted almost of its own volition. Not a major hit, not a punch, just a slap, and a relatively gentle one at that. The mark it had left was gone almost as soon as it had appeared, lost in the reddening marks of Judy's own fury.

"You can't get on with anyone, can you?" she had screamed at him, throwing his clothes at him in great ratted armfuls. "You rile everyone you meet, piss everyone off, make yourself hateful to everyone, you scratch at them till they haven't got a choice but to hate you and to cut you out of their life, and now even I hate you. Are you satisfied? *Are* you?" She had pushed at him then, pushed him past the bedroom where they had made love and the sofa where they had cuddled and the kitchen where they had cooked together and once laid upon the floor and ate each other and finally forced him through the door. He had not raised his hand to her again, frightened of his own actions but more frightened of her aggressive response. He had gone meekly, excised from her life as cleanly as a plucked hair or loosed turd.

Once he pulled back the uppermost blankets, the bed was mostly clean and Parnell sat on it, his knees drawn up tight and his arms wrapped around his legs. The room was warm, far warmer than the paltry heating system had managed the previous night, but the warmth now was fevered and prickling. It carried the moisture on its lips, the air sweating onto him in fetid, dank waves. Shadows crept around the edges of the room, slick and weeping. Although he saw nothing moving, the walls seemed to swell when he turned away; the moss sucking its way across the floor and tiny bubbles of fungus appearing whenever he looked around. And there were noises.

It was as though something was breathing, not near him or

far from him but all around him, great rattling exhalations and inhalations that sounded like the gurgles of lungs that were clotted with blood or pus. The walls themselves seemed to groan in response to the breathing, creaking like canvas under pressure, and Parnell could almost see them expanding as they did so, swelling like baking bread into the room. There was another sound, of something flowing and pulsing, that came from beyond the door and walls. It was the sound of liquid tumbling and driven, and all the while the temperature rose and the smell in the room grew worse. Parnell was reminded of the smell of hospitals, not the antiseptic smell of the wards, no, this was the smell that sat underneath that—the corrupted and blighted smell of illness, of things rotting and of flesh unable to win the uneven battle between itself and decay.

Even as he watched, more moss bloomed in the room. The door warped, creaking, so that Parnell doubted he would be able to open it again. Besides, the walls had swollen further, creating a loose lip that lay over the frame. Everything in the room was being slowly submerged by walls and a floor that looked soft and doughy. Parnell had a sudden vivid image of the hotel as a living thing and himself as an infection, an irritant to be dealt with, and he shuddered. All day, he had been attacking the hotel, had been doing it really since he arrived yesterday, drawing attention to himself, making himself noticeable. He wondered who the message writer really was. Some other poor sod, pulled here but who had worked things out earlier, learned not to be so obvious in the hope that the hotel left them alone? Some element of his own mind, warning him? He had no idea, but he hoped it was another person. Knowing that someone else was close, was suffering just like he was, helped. Around him, the room closed in.

The gap around the doorway was closing to a clenched throat when Parnell realised he had to move. The room was getting smaller and smaller as the walls and floor swelled. Yellowing liquid was weeping from the surfaces, dripping down and pooling across the floor in a vile slick, and the fungal growths had started popping out in the centre of the liquid as though it were feeding them. Whatever the rest of the hotel was like, it surely could not be any worse than this. Parnell stepped down gingerly from the bed and lurched, his foot sinking immediately into the floor. Unbalanced, he wobbled and fell, landing on his hands and knees and sinking several inches down into the terrible, sucking wet. He screamed, partly in panic and partly because it *burned*, an acidic rasp that attacked his skin. He thrashed, and the floor thrashed back at him, its surface convulsing violently. Black moss flowed out from around his wrists and up his arms, and kissed sickly against his legs. He opened his mouth to scream but the moss had already reached his face, was filling his mouth. He tasted something beyond foul and tried to spit but it was thick and cloying. Yellow liquid spattered across him as the floor bucked again and he sank deeper, feeling the fevered heat of its depths. He glimpsed the room, seen through a yellow glaze as the liquid covered his face, saw the fungus growing on *him,* spores clinging to his skin, and then the wall had swollen enough to touch him, was sucking at him. Parnell struggled to free himself one more time but the room refused to let him go and then he was covered completely and there was no light left and he sank inside the heated, accepting flesh.

The hotel devoured him.

THE KNITTED CHILD

THIS IS WHAT it knew:

When the old woman's granddaughter's menses came again, there had been tears and grief. The old woman, punctured by the granddaughter's loss but seeing that her shoulders could bear no more sorrow than the weight they were already carrying, had gone as quickly as her age would allow to her room. She went folded in on herself, her shoulder-blades sticking out like crow's wings, her spindle arms and tree-twig hands no defence against the digging pain in her own belly. The long-forgotten memory of her own bleeding out returned with a terrible clarity and she had remembered then, remembered all the life she had carried inside herself and lost in her earlier years, remembered the pain, remembered the hopes that shrivelled as they were exposed to the air. Remembered about loss. She had held herself clenched until she was back in her room and then she allowed her own tears to come, and when they did, they were hot and heavy and danced like flies upon her cheeks. Sitting in her chair, she finally allowed her own grief to hold court, and it ruled her with fists of thick, wringing iron.

Later, the old woman's daughter had come into the room, without knocking and without smiling. The old woman had stopped crying by then but the marks of her tears were still clear in the swell of her eyes and the droplet stains across the clothing that covered her drydust chest.

"What's wrong with you?" her daughter asked, so like her father. "You haven't lost anything; neither's she, has she? All this fuss! Anyone'd think someone's died, and they've not, have they? Not really. Anyway, they'll try again." And she had busied herself with cleaning, even though the old woman did not want her to. She had not tried to explain to her daughter, to make her understand; the girl was stubborn and practical like her father, but less tolerant and less pleasant and quicker to spur into argument. The old woman loved her with all her heart but she did not, try as she might, like her very much and she did not want to talk to her then. Instead, she had waited until her daughter had gone and then she took her knitting needles and wool from her bedside table, removing the half-finished baby blanket from the needles and unstitched it carefully, unravelling the fawn lamb's wool and then had cast on, winding the soft fabric around her needles.

The old woman's hands were gnarled from arthritis and no longer had the delicacy to do her beloved embroidery. Knitting was still within her reach, however, as long as the patterns were not complicated and the stitches required were large. The thing she started to knit that morning was simple, an easy arrangement of stitch and thread and filling that fell from her needles and into being as smoothly as silk from worms. She had knitted all day and long into the night, the heartbeat rhythm of the needles filling her room like tidal water until eventually, she was finished. From the first stitch, tying thread to thread, the old woman had let her needles caper and weave, ignoring the pain that scoured her knuckles and that burned like white fire in the wasting flesh of her wrists because this was creation; she was knitting against loss, was knitting hope.

The old woman was old, and her magic was mostly gone and that which remained was weary and brittle, but it was all she had, so she fed it down along the clacking needles and swinging yarn, let it mingle and take form and hoped it might flower. Slow at first and then faster, the stitches clumsy and uneven but solid and sure all the same, the thing was brought forth. The old woman had given it two arms and two legs, and a mouth and eyes, and the most basic of ears and for its flesh she used fibres that rustled as she filled its body and tickled the inside of its skin as she stitched it closed. It came into existence with the knowledge that it could not grow, had no hands to hold out nor voice to speak its feelings, but it had love to give, and solace and tenderness, and it wanted to belong. This is what it knew.

The old woman's granddaughter was young and the knitted child saw she must have been pretty before the sobbing took hold and bled her eyes raw and sagged her skin into folds. It saw her first the morning after her blood came, when the family ate their breakfast together. They were seated around her in frail near-silence, only the old woman's daughter talking as though life went on when clearly, just for that morning, it had stopped. The granddaughter's husband, big-boned and florid, kept his own grief inside him with bands of iron will but it was still written clear on his face. He patted her hand often as they sat at the breakfast table; when he did, she flinched as though she could not bear to be touched by anyone. When he tried to hug her and kiss her cheek, she turned away and shut her eyes, closing herself off from him and the rest of the family. The knitted child watched from the old woman's bag as first the daughter and then one by one the other members of the household left, with the husband the last to go, slump-shouldered and silent. It was only then that the old woman brought the knitted child out, and handed it over.

"For you," she said. "A child. For you." The old woman's granddaughter took the child, knitted in fine wool of different colours, its knitstitch eyes glittering and its mouth a ragged, closed line in a face that showed no expression, and held it. Her hands were cold and trembling, shaking the knitted child in a tarantella palsy and there was little but stuffing and hope in the child, the hope of wanting to love and be loved and it stared at the granddaughter so that she would know this, would feel it, and waited until she finally drew it into a hug as tight as gritted teeth.

The granddaughter did not let the knitted child away from her for the whole day, carrying him draped into the crook of her left arm or right as she carried out her chores, and sitting him on her lap when she ate her lunch. The child gloried in her warmth and tried to keep his woollen skin from scratching her bare arms. When it sat in her lap, it enjoyed the press of her belly and the feel of her womb under her skin and it took in her smell and the feel of her. *I am yours*, it wanted to say, *I am the child you wished for, made real by needle and loss and love and stitch, and I shall love you now and always,* but it had no choice but to keep the words inside itself and only hope its mother could feel them through the cloying layers of her unhappiness.

The old woman stayed with the granddaughter during the day and saw that things between her and the knitted child were well and finally allowed herself a smile, her first since the coming of the blood. It was an old smile, the knitted child saw, careworn at the edges and shallow. Her grief, though, was gone, tied into the child's skin by the pattern of interlocked stitch and thread, taken from the old woman morsel by morsel until she could still taste it but did not feel the congealed weight of it in her stomach. Her grief was lost in the knitted child's stuffing belly, and it took it gladly.

The granddaughter wept for most of the day, sometimes running a hand over her stomach as though to soothe an ache, or clutching her new child to herself even more tightly. When she finished her chores she took to her bed and rested, lying on her soft mattress and continuing to weep. Her tears, fuller than the old woman's but sharper, dripped across the knitted child's face and for a moment they sat, glistening and loose, on its own eyes and it looked up at her through a skin of water. Then, sucked in by the knitted child's need, the tears soaked away to nothing, becoming thinner and thinner until they were gone completely and it felt, for the shortest of times, that it was being born, was rising through the granddaughter's waters to take its place at her side. It wished that the old woman had given it muscles, fingers, lips that were not bound to each other, so that it could reach out and hold the granddaughter, stroke her hair, tell her that all things would be well because it was here now and it loved her. Instead, it took her tears into itself and put them with the old woman's grief, deep in its centre, where they could be held tight and close and private.

The granddaughter would not eat her food that night either. Despite the old woman and her daughter's persuasions, she merely curled into a tight ball on her bed, arms and legs bunched close like tangled vines and the knitted child wrapped in that aching flesh. She would not talk, and looked only at the child.

"You can try again," the daughter said, and "It's only another month," and "It's hardly any time since you married," and "Sometimes these things don't come easy" and, finally,

"Life goes on". The old woman simply said, "Let it out, child" and patted the granddaughter's head and stroked her in a way that the knitted child could not and that made the twists in its stomach tighten in helpless misery. The granddaughter did not reply to either of them.

Even the granddaughter's husband could not bring her to speech except for the most simple of conversations, though he sat with her for the whole evening after his return from work and spoke to her about his day and the future and the past and plans both possible and unlikely. He tried to lay a raw hand upon her shoulders but she moved away, leaving him sitting on the edge of the bed with the hand hovering in the air like some pale, fat bird that could find nowhere to land. Tears gathered in his eyes and he said, "I feel it too," but the granddaughter ignored him and the knitted child closed itself to his pain. The man made no mention of the knitted child, and the knitted child dismissed him. Its mother was hurting, and it loved her and she was its world and all that mattered. It was its mother's child, and had no father.

It came to know the patterns in the life it had been born to, to recognise the routines that ebbed and flowed from day to day and that carried them all along in their bobbing, all-embracing wake. Mornings were rushed, flurries of activity breaking out across the house as the daughter made breakfast for the rest of the household, as beds were stripped or rooms prepared for cleaning, as the men (the granddaughter's husband and the daughter's husband and her son) ate and then went to work, and as the old woman was helped with her morning toilet. Towards lunch, the house relaxed, quieter without the men and with the chores mostly complete, the women's movement slowing but never stopping until finally, after lunch, they had time to attend to themselves. All through those days, through the restlessness of tasks and the lacunae of quieter moments, the granddaughter carried the knitted child, shifting it from arm to arm to accommodate her activity as it carried her pain for her, a cold, bilious and ragged thing in its chest.

On the seventh night, when the knitted child was growing to recognise even the tiniest shifts of its mother's moods by the sound of her voice and the way her body felt against its own, her husband came to talk to her and the child felt her stiffen. The husband spoke of moving on, of trying again, of letting things go that she was holding too tight, and he sounded like the old woman's daughter as he spoke, as though he were a mouthpiece of flesh and bone speaking only what was relayed to him. He had said similar things the previous nights, and each night she had ignored him and he had eventually left her to her weeping. That night, however, he would not walk away.

"It's not healthy. You have to let it go," the husband said and the knitted child took several long moments before it realised that he was talking about *it*, about its mother abandoning it. *No*, it wanted to say, *I am not some scrap to be discarded like kitchen waste, I am her child.*

I am her child.

"I know she made it for you to help you get over what happened, but never letting it go isn't healthy. It's not the answer. It was a terrible thing, terrible for both of us, but we have to stay positive, not become lost to each other. We have to believe that we can do this. We have to believe that we can try again and that we'll be successful," the husband carried on. "That thing isn't a child," and the knitted child's moveless mouth shrieked at what it heard, no sound emerging, echoing instead around the stuffed caverns of its body. The granddaughter cried when she heard her husband, tears that tasted different than those that had come before, raw and salty and tender as scraped flesh. She tried to move across her bed away from her husband but he came along with her, giving her no space, cloistering her and the knitted child with his bulk and the sweat not yet dry on his skin, and his smell of labour and ache and need and determination. The granddaughter wept bitterly, saying "It loves me" and her husband replied, "It can't, my sweet." The knitted child screamed his silent scream once more.

"Please," the granddaughter said. "Please."

"It's a fucking doll," the husband said, his voice as quiet as frost in the bedroom. "Keep it if you want; I know your grandmother made it and that she means well and that it has helped you these last days, but please, you have to let it go."

"But it loves me," the granddaughter repeated and the knitted child wished again for a mouth so that he could add his voice to theirs, to say that, *yes*, he did love her and he could come to love the husband in time, as the husband would surely love him if only he was allowed to remain. The old woman's magic writhed in it, corpse-dry and weak and feverish, made of love sweetened by grief and misery.

The husband left then, and the granddaughter cried yet more tears. The husband did not stay away for long; when he returned, he carried with him wine and two glasses and the granddaughter at first merely looked at him and clutched the knitted child tighter than she had ever done. It bloomed with joy to think that she had decided to carry on holding it, to keep it close to her, that she loved it and *oh Mother I love you!* And then, with the slow deliberation of an infant taking the first steps that the knitted child could only dream of, the granddaughter placed the child on the floor beside the bed and held out her arms to her husband.

The wine was gone and the room was soaked with darkness but the granddaughter and the husband were not quiet.

It could not see them from its place on the floor, but it heard them as they shifted and wept and laughed and talked. The child was cold and it missed its mother's embrace and it wanted to call for her, to plead for her return, but its mouth would not move and it had no air to make words. Instead, it lay and listened as the granddaughter and her husband locked each other in the rhythmic touch of forgetting and creating and looking forward, and the sound of its heart breaking was vast and silent.

THE DRUNKS' TOTEM

THE MORNING THAT Fuchs saw the sculpture, he had
lost twenty-four of his sixty kilogram target and was
aiming to walk two miles.

It was in the centre of the grass, hidden from view by the
trees until he came around the curve of the path; branches
and twigs twisted together and planted into the earth,
thrusting into the still-dark sky and moving in the breeze.
The outermost ends of the branches and twigs were adorned
with bottles and bags, giving it the look of a skeletal thing
grown bulbous, budding. It startled Fuchs, made him jump
when he saw it and then laugh at himself for his nervousness.

Fuchs was fat. Not overweight or large or chunky, but fat.
Obese, actually. "You aren't morbidly obese," said his doctor,
Longdon, during his last appointment, "but it's only a matter
of time. Your joints are struggling, your blood pressure and
cholesterol are high and God only knows the toll it's taking
on your heart and lungs." Longdon had said more, giving
Fuchs diet sheets and exercise advice leaflets, all of which
Fuchs intended to ignore, had it not been for Longdon's last
comment.

"The question is, what do you want to see when you look in the mirror? The physical things, the fatness and the joints and the blood pressure, are remarkably easy to sort out, but it's your mind that has to change. You have to *want* it. Look at yourself tonight in the mirror and decide—are these the eyes I want?" Fuchs had done as he asked that evening, looking, *really* looking, at himself in his shaving mirror. His eyes were flat pools, dark with exhausted shadows, yet when he looked at himself in his childhood photographs that lined his walls, he had happy, vibrant eyes. In his childhood photographs he was thin and happy and living, and he wanted to be that again. Not all of it, certainly; not thin, particularly, but with living eyes that did not look reptilian in their misery. He wanted a chance of happiness.

As he walked, the sculpture stood sentinel to his side. Its twisted limbs writhed and reached out to him, dancing in the stiffening wind that swept in from the estuary. In the moonlight, its swollen fingers made obscene passes through the air, rich with dank intimation and disquieting, fleshy promises. The local drunks had made it, Fuchs presumed, telling the story of their night's activities through this weird totem. It wasn't the first time that he had come across their leavings—bottles and cans, the blackened remains of fires, sometimes clothes and once the remains of a sleeping bag, its skin slashed and its filling strewn across the ground in sodden white clumps. Normally, the drunks were gone by the time he arrived, only occasionally remaining there to jeer at him as he shuffled along, their cries settling on his broad and wobbling shoulders. He hated them because they frightened him and because they laughed at him and because he could do nothing about either.

So, exercise and diet. Diet was easy; Fuchs simply replaced as much of his current food with low fat alternatives as he could. Exercise was harder. Strenuous exercise was out, both Longdon and Fuchs agreed on that. Swimming, favoured by Longdon, was out as well; Fuchs was acutely conscious of his flabby body, and revealing it near-naked in public was unthinkable. "So get a good pair of training shoes and a sweat suit and walk," said Longdon, and Fuchs had done just that and in doing so found the solitary activity he needed. When walking, he could hide in the night and still get fit and no one need see him.

Fuchs' preferred place to walk was the local cycle track. It was an oval of concrete path encircling grassed playing fields and abutting the river, built on reclaimed ground that never felt truly dry. Trees surrounded it, and mostly, it was deserted during the pre-dawn hours Fuchs spent there. The only illumination that reached the track was the cool glamour of the stars and the moon and the ambient light from the distant town, bleeding the air a musty orange and glittering across the surface of the river that washed itself alongside the straightest section of the path. Fuchs was starting along that section now, the path unravelling ahead of him, a lighter strip of grey in the gloom. There was no movement, no noise. No drunks. Mists rose from the river, its level raised by the tide so that it lapped at the uppermost edges of the ground which sloped away from the path and completely swallowed the silt flats that lay between the path and the water. He liked the sound of the river as he walked, enjoyed its gentle lap and suck. He usually liked its smell too, a fresh tang of salt and clean mud that washed the faint smells of exhaust fumes and cheap takeaways from the air.

This morning, however, it smelled wrong.

It was a rich odour, pungent with brine and rottenness and something else, something like fish gone bad and houses long abandoned, and pale, stagnant water. It made the air heavy, a syrupy thing that clogged Fuchs' lungs and left his teeth furred with loose tracks of slime. Grimacing, he tried to breathe through his mouth but he could still smell it, could *feel* it slithering around his tongue and down his throat. He wondered about turning back, cutting short his walk, but did not want to. This was his time, precious to him in ways he could not easily articulate. He had been here in every type of weather, in summer and, like now, in the depths of winter, and had never yet missed a day or failed to complete the tasks he set himself; he had left his fat strewn along the length of these paths, bundled in healthy sweat and his own growing pride.

Besides, turning back meant going past the construction of branches and the thought of that made him as uneasy as braving the smell. It was the sculpture's angularity that bothered him, as though it were mocking him with its scrawniness. Looking back, Fuchs saw that it was still there, just visible in the darkness, its legs and arms blurring into the mist. *Legs?* he snapped at himself. *Arms? And why shouldn't it still be there? Where would it have gone?* It was just a stupid joke, just a lurching, creeping thing in the dark.

Now, why had he thought 'creeping'? It couldn't creep, couldn't move at all. It was simply branches and rubbish, twisted into a shape almost like a living thing. Fuchs set his back to it and walked on.

The smell became worse as he walked, thickening into the air and laying against his sweating skin in slippery, tangled skeins. What *was* it? A cow, perhaps, washed down from the farmlands upriver, bloated and swollen in death? Pollution, oil or rendering from the slaughterhouse on the outskirts of the town? It came in waves, rising but not falling away, seeding the air with the scents not just of death but of *wrongness*, of corruption and blight.

And then something moved in the water. Fuchs did not see it; the darkness shifted about him as ever, the moon dancing behind clouds and reappearing, but he heard it. There was a splash as the something pressed against the current, breaking the surface of the river. Below the splash there was another noise, a great exhalation that carried the suggestion but not the sound of language within it. The river noises were lost for a moment beneath nearly-heard words that were in no recognisable tongue and which itched at Fuchs' ears. He peered intently across the expanse of water and had a momentary impression of a disruption in the rippling, reflected light that played across the water's surface. There was a great shifting of a mass that he could not identify and then, with another splash, it was gone.

The smell faded with it. *Perhaps,* thought Fuchs, *it had been a cow after all, caught on something and splitting with decay.* Shifting currents had finally moved it on, letting the air trapped within it escape in a foul, sussurant belch. It made sense; he had been spooked by the sculpture and then over-reacted to a noise from the river. Just a fat man jumping at shadows. He walked on, angry at himself.

A little further along, Fuchs came across cans scattered across the path and down the slope to the river. They were not the normal detritus of Lancaster's midnight drinkers, crumpled and pockmarked with cigarette burns. Instead, these had been twisted and torn into new shapes, tiny homunculi with grasping hands and clawed, supplicant fingers. Some bobbed on the surface of the water, shadowed and glistening with moisture. As he watched, one slipped below the surface with a faint *plop* of bubbled air. It did not resurface. On some of the cans closest to him, Fuchs saw that the edges of the torn metal were crusted with a blackness that might be blood but which looked somehow thicker and less vital. In their posture the cans looked helpless, laid out in sacrifice and desperate for rescue. Fuchs moved through them as quickly as he could, lurching like a newly-mobile toddler as he tried to maintain his speed whilst not touching the wretched figures. They shifted in the breeze as he passed, spinning as though trying to follow him and silently beseeching him for help.

Fuchs had reached the halfway point of the straight length of path now. To one side, the river moved in slow crests; to the other was a playing field whose grass caught the low moonlight in grey pools. Wreathed in mist, its surface was churned and split, the earth's dark flesh showing through in glistening whorls. The pattern of the scarring was strange, Fuchs saw. It looked disjointed, but there seemed to be a pattern there, an underlying meaning in those exposed swirls that was just out of his reach. Not words, certainly; an older and more guttural communication full of brutal plosives and glottal stops, given form in text and etched on the ground's very skin. The scars seemed to writhe as he looked at them, changing their meaning in aching, clutching instants. Fuchs turned furiously away telling himself, "Nonsense."

Beyond the grass a fringe of trees stood, alert in the night. The hectic dance of their limbs in the wind sent rustles of sound to him and shadows slipped around their trunks, leaning out to reach for him across the open space. The trees looked sickly in the reluctant light, stunted and bowed by the weight of the darkness. Creeping shadows joined with the churned earth, surrounding him, trapping him in the night's tongues. He wanted to be home now, to be away from here and he walked more quickly, forcing his protesting legs to greater speed despite the roaring in his joints and the ragged stab of breath in his lungs.

He saw another totem ahead of him, this one planted out

in the river itself. It rose from the water a few feet from the
bank, its bony limbs hung with strips of cloth that fluttered
madly in the breeze. It was bigger than the first, taller and
more solid. Fuchs had the sudden, awful feeling that it was a
purposeful creation, not a mere drunken fancy. It was an
indicator, although of what, he did not know. A calling,
perhaps, or a request, urgent and ragged with longing. More
sacrificial cans floated around it, along with what appeared
to be dead fish and pages torn from a book. The sodden
paper had swelled in the water and were bleached the
shredded, dirty ivory of old tusks. Shivering as the water
pressed around it, the totem lurched at Fuchs as he came
abreast of it. He cried out, turned his face down so that he
would not see the thing, and hurried on. For the first time in
his adult life, Fuchs forced himself to run.

Dark lines curled around Fuchs' feet as he moved, shadows
which made impossible shapes and capering around him like
antic worms grown fat on diseased soil. His shuffling feet
dragged through them, feeling a resistance to his passage that
was impossible but was real, and only his great weight helped
him overcome. Air wheezed in and out of his lungs, each
exhalation spattering saliva out past his lips and each
inhalation sucking sharp pains in with it. His heart throbbed
and his belly shook as spasms nipped at his gross flesh,
sending ripples playing across his skin. He floundered,
slowing, his mass the victor in the uneven battle with his
strength. Raising his head, he saw that he was close to the
edge of the fringe of trees, where the path began to move
away from the river. Lost in the darkness of the tree trunks,
more totems danced their slow, gathering dance.

Stopping was as hard as running; Fuchs ceased moving his
legs but carried on forwards and stumbled, the bulk of his
body still shifting, dragging his weight over and past the

balancing point of his already protesting knees. He took several helpless steps towards the beckoning figures before he came to a complete stop, air rattling in his ears and scouring his throat. The moon, freshly appeared from behind the scudding clouds, elongated the shadows further, draping them up his legs and dappling his belly and chest. The shadows lay across him like bloated fingers, grasping and tugging at him in a boneless caress.

From this close, Fuchs could see differences between the totems. Some were tall, made of larger branches and fringed with twigs and paper or material left to dangle and dance as the air shifted about them; others were smaller, seemingly fashioned from rubbish or smaller pieces of the trees, hunched low to the ground like scurrying things dragged from absolute darkness and desperate to be back in its embrace. Here and there, more of the tiny figures made from cans dangled from outstretched limbs, twisting in the air and catching, reflecting, losing the moon's graceful light. Yet more lay strewn about the floor, writhing as the wind caught them up and then dropped them again. Even the trees themselves looked to have been twisted into unnatural shapes, their trunks forced around and their limbs brought out so that they made half-human figures but with too many arms, more fingers than any human could have, endlessly grasping at the air, at him.

No, not grasping. The shadows might feel as though they were gripping at him, but the figures did not. Rather, he felt that they were calling, their sinuous movements an endless invocation, but from whom and to what? Not him, of that he was sure. They reached past him, over him and around towards the river and, beyond it, to the sea with its abyssal depths and cold, swirling currents. Reached and called, a summoning in the same language he had seen etched into the grass and mud, in a voice both vast and chill. Fuchs looked back along the path, at the other totem now almost hidden in the glittering mists, its feet lost to the water and yet its message no less immediate. It, too, bent supplicant in the wind to the expanse of water beyond. Past it, invisible now, the first figure he had seen still danced, he was sure, still called out with urgent clenches of its bony, ragged fingers. Fuchs, his mind faster than his body could ever hope to be, understood without knowing how that he had fallen into the centre of a great invocation, some ceremony whose design and purpose was unclear but which he felt, *knew*, to be wrong.

Around him, the wind shifted once again, bringing with it once more the sound of those corrupted and bitter words. They were desperate now, building towards a frenzy that capered about his ears and prickled at his head. Sounds like the bubbling of ocean slime and the roaring of approaching beasts played around him, catching in his hearing and at his throat with pallid mutterings. And then he saw what bobbed in the water further out into the river.

At first, he thought they were fallen totems, broken collections of branches whose paler wooden flesh showed gleaming against the darker skin of bark, but then he saw more clearly the shapes of the floating things and saw the ivory gleaming for the bone it was. Flesh, teased into corrupt patterns, clung to the bone and drifted in eddies at the river's surface. On some pieces, fur was visible; on others, shreds of clothing lay across the exposed meat and entangled in the water alongside them. The bodies were mangled, torn and savaged and even in the constantly shifting light, Fuchs saw that there were curious marks and bruises across the exposed skin. Whorls and curves covered it, the edges of great circles, puckered and ripped and dried to a weeping crust, the imprint of violence whose cause he could neither identify nor name. Horrified, Fuchs lurched back. The moon, gliding behind more cloud and softening the shadows into a messy, jigging confusion of overlapping, distorting edges, covered the slaughterhouse remains with a shroud's pallor.

He took another step, feeling exposed as he backed away from the river. His heels kicked against the prostrate can men, the sound of their skittering harsh and shrill against the staccato swirl of the angry sounds that still shimmered around him. What in the name of God had happened here? There looked to be many bodies out in the water, animals as well as people. Fuchs wanted to think that they had been the victim of a frenzied human assault, but something about the torn and tattered flesh put him in mind of animal attacks, great crescents of muscle exposed by a shark's teeth or an alligator's fangs. Surely no man could have done that? Another step away from the terror of it; another. Another, and more cans clattered about his feet.

Another, and he saw movement at the edge of his vision.

Across the expanse of grass, over the etched earth, shapes moved in the shadows and darted among the trees. Creeping figures slipped from behind trunk to behind trunk, graceful and silent in the darkness. What light there was, hazy moonshine saturated by cloud and the dwelling lights in the distance, reflected on the shuddering surface of the river, hesitated at the treeline. Fuchs could not see clearly, but the figures looked as though they were *dancing*, gyrating as they darted from hiding place to hiding place, their arms flailing and their feet leaving the earth for seconds at a time as they leapt in graceless bounds. They came no further than the edge of the trees, sometimes allowing themselves to be caught by the light, their pale nudity exposed and then lost again as they cavorted back. Fuchs had the impression of saliva strings trailing down chests, of mud spattering across legs, of hair twisted with sweat and dirt. Of branches and cans held aloft and waved as though in obscene greeting.

Of hands, slick with blood.

Whoever they were, Fuchs knew that they were not drunks; these were no stumbling inebriates jeering from afar and mocking with thoughtless cruelty. There was a purpose to their movements, a rhythm evident in their revealing themselves to him and then slipping into the shadows again that was intended to scare him. That they were the creators of the totems, he had no doubt; their fevered dancing seemed to be a moving mirror for the totems' ragged, twisting shapes. He had never felt more exposed, standing between the cold reaches of the river and the frantic, dervish movements and the leering attention of the totems ahead and behind him. He turned, peering into the darkness around him in hope of some avenue of escape, but none presented itself. The dancers were getting closer, coming further out from the cover of the trees before they darted back into the inky shadows, and although he could not see their eyes he knew that they were fixed on him with a glittering, hungry intensity. Around them, the chanted words came stronger, peaking in dry staccato bursts and longer moist phrases and in a moment he realised that the dancers were not uttering the words themselves but rather, the very earth was sounding the words written upon it, letting them rise from the ground like dank mist that swirled up in a great cry of desperate summoning.

Before Fuchs could even wonder why the sounds made him think of a summoning, there was another sound, this time from the river. A splash, and then a writhing, heaving noise as if something huge was being dragged through the mud at the water's edge. Or was dragging itself from the water. He stood motionless, hoping to still his breathing, become a fat statue invisible in the darkness but aware of the hot glow of observation from in amongst the trees.

Another noise, a rattling of cans as they skittered across the earth and the path and knocked together. Then, a moment later, the sound of water breaking and spraying. The smell came again, fierce as burning spices and then the words rose up further, gibbering, insistent, barely audible but louder than any other sound in his life. Fuchs stared back along the path and saw a black shape pulsate at the river's edge, saw the flailing of things that he wanted to believe were arms but knew were not and heard the terrible, dark grunting as it thrust itself forward again. More cans scattered before it and the water behind it rippled and thrashed as it heaved again. The not-arms flailed, slapping down into the mud and across the path, great ropes of flesh that glistened in the dark with water and movement. One whipped out further, digging into the earth on the far side of the path, and a trembling moan rose from the people in the trees; anticipatory, desperate, longing. The thing in the water grunted again, the sound of air being expelled through lips that were the wrong shape and size to form simple words. Another heave, and more of its body appeared, humped and dripping in the night. Fuchs, still frozen in fear, had a momentary glimpse of other things buried in the water beyond, clawing at the surface only to fall back again with splashes like dark chuckles.

No, not *more* things; one massive thing, its flesh filling the whole of the river, pulling itself up upon the shore increment by tiny increment. Its not-arms (*tentacles*, he said to himself, *tentacles*) thrashed, gripping at the concrete and earth and tightening like the steel hawsers of a ship docked in a storm. Another shudder of movement and the vast body crept another few inches forwards, mud splaying out from under it as more of it came ashore. A huge eye, black as lost hopes, peered at him as voices raised themselves in triumphant howls and then Fuchs was running.

He knew within a few steps that it was not going to work; pain, fresh and sharp, exploded in his knees at every step. His fat, the outlying regions of his body that he had so recently started to shed, moved against the rhythm of his lumbering run, disrupting his balance, pulling him one way and then the other, and his lungs clenched and roared in violent rebellion to the exertion. But, mostly, it was that he was too slow.

Never before had Fuchs felt his size and the ungainliness of his body so acutely. No matter what messages, borne of terror, he sent to his legs they could not carry him any faster away from the emerging thing. His muscles pushed and his survival instinct roared but his body, so long his enemy, now became his undoing. He could feel the air move at his back, hear the writhing language curl around, pulling the thing in the river into existence, felt the gaze of the impossible thing upon him as the tentacles sliced the air at his shoulder and bit into the ground at either side of him. They dragged gouges into the soil as they grew taut and the noise of a great mass dragging itself further up the slope came to him in a sour wave. Leaping figures bounded across the field to his side, and more were even now pushing their way through the trees ahead of him, kicking at the ground and shaking the totems so that they, too, became part of the dance, their bony limbs jerking in spastic anticipation. From behind there was more noise, a huffed exhalation that broke around him in a damp, stinking caress. The figures danced on, more and more frenzied, urging the thing behind him to keep coming and Fuchs fled and knew that he could not flee.

It was his left knee that finally gave up the uneven struggle. It cracked with the sound of a stout branch wrenched from a dying tree, and Fuchs crashed over, slammed hard into the ground and rolled onto his back. A great scream loosed itself from him as he thrashed, the pain from his leg a white-hot glare in the darkness. He struggled over onto his front, knowing it was hopeless but crawling on anyway, his hands digging into the earth and his feet scrabbling for purchase. More tentacles slapped to the floor around him, more huffing and panting sounds rolled across him and the dancers came ever closer, penning him inside a writhing, wailing circle.

A tentacle fell across his shoulder. Gripped, tightened. Dug in, and drew him back towards the river. He twisted and rolled, trying to break its grip until another tentacle whipped around his legs and a further one slipped around his belly with a touch a subtle as a lover's finger before digging cruelly tight. Weeping, he cursed his slow and bloated flesh as behind him something grand and ancient pulled itself from the river and came to feed.

Implementing the Least Desirable Solution

"**I**T'S VERY IMPRESSIVE."

"Thank you, sir. It's a state of the art facility I think you can be proud of."

"You misunderstand, Dr Morris. I mean that the amount of money you have spent is impressive, for very little return. We have bankrolled this establishment and several expeditions, we cover the huge and ongoing running costs, and yet we have little to show for it besides the creature itself."

"Yes."

"And then, of course, there's the compensation."

"Yes."

"How many has it killed so far?"

"In total? Eight. Five on the expedition, one more in transit and two whilst it's been here."

"And how many prior to its capture?"

"I don't know."

"Don't you?"

"No. I'm sorry, we never thought to check. Quite a few

over the years, certainly, natives and early explorers. We think. It's hard to know."

"I see. Well, Dr Morris, improvements are required. We expect results soon."

"Yes."

"Soon, Dr Morris. Or we shall be forced to review our involvement in this work and your part in it."

"Yes. I understand."

"Good. Soon, Dr Morris."

"Yes."

"Soon."

Morris licked his lips when he was nervous, and was annoyed to find that he was still licking them hours after the money man had gone, driving his unobtrusive little car back along the snaking road that led through the village and to the nearby town. Soon, he had said, but how was he supposed to achieve it? You couldn't rush this kind of work. Not here, and not under these circumstances.

Morris' office was built so that one wall was dominated by a huge window that faced out into the creature's enclosure. When the facility had been at the design stage, before all of this had become so *real*, Morris had argued that it would give him the chance to study the creature even when they were not actually testing it, and whilst that was certainly true, it wasn't the real reason he had demanded its construction. No, that had been his way of showing his authority. *I'm here,* it said to all the doubters and naysayers, *I'm here and I'm here to stay, so get used to it.* Only, he couldn't really say that because of the secrecy levels attached to the project and besides, the office didn't feel safe any more.

It was the creature's fault. Ever since the aborted first

attempt at capture on the tenth day of the expedition, when it had torn apart one of the porters and a junior field scientist called Henry Summers, it had proved to be so much *more* than they anticipated. Even before then, tracking it had proved a near-impossible nightmare of lost trails, harsh terrain and false starts. The attack on their camp the night after Summers' death had been an unexpected move on its behalf, indicating a capacity for both vengeful thinking and planning, which they had not believed it possessed. Morris could easily, *too* easily, recall the sound of it hissing as men screamed, recall the feel of his own urine pooling under his buttocks as he remained, silent and trembling, in his tent. He could still remember the rain of what turned out to be blood spattering on the outside of the canvas, its hollow drumming a counterpoint to his heartbeat. The attack had lasted sixteen minutes; sixteen minutes that had felt like a frenzied age, and when the creature went, it took with it most of one of their porters and left two more strewn around the campsite in pieces; they found one of the poor bastard's heads pushed so far down into the mud that only his eyes and forehead showed, the stump of his torn neck entirely submerged. A fourth man would never walk again, and a fifth needed feeding through a tube and made moaning sounds that were probably the closest to screams he could manage. It had been a mess, pure and simple, and the blame had been placed at Morris' door, which he felt was unfair. How could he have known?

Even when they managed to get it into the cage and onto the transport boat (disguised as a tramp cargo ship, allowing them to sail back in under the noses of their competitors and rivals; Morris' idea, and about the only one during the entire expedition which had worked well), the damned thing had proved almost unmanageable, escaping twice and killing one crew member during the course of the voyage. It was fast, they had known that, but it was smart as well; it had a knack with locks and puzzles that meant it twice worked out how to open its cage, both times when most of the crew were asleep and when the moves to recapture it were slow and confused. Coincidence, or planning on the creature's part? It was difficult to know, back then at least. Now, he was sure that there were no coincidences, not a single one.

After the second time, Morris had ordered its cage welded shut and that had held it. The body of the sailor had been left inside the cage; no one wanted to risk entering to retrieve it and besides, it had meant they didn't have to feed the creature for the remainder of the journey.

All the way from the dock to the lab (disguised as a food additives research laboratory and located in the hills above a village whose population was in the low hundreds), Morris had worried. What if it got out again? Were they right to risk keeping it alive? He had argued forcefully that killing the creature was the least desirable option, that alive it represented a better source of material for research. It would certainly be easier to handle dead, but it was also finite, would run out eventually. Alive, they could learn from its behaviour, link activity to chemistry, make a fortune by adapting, synthesising, processing, patenting and then marketing what they found. In the end, his wisdom had prevailed. The least desirable option had been shelved, and the creature was allowed to remain alive.

And now? Now they had it here, and none of the things they tried to do were working.

In the days after the money man's visit, Morris ordered a range of repeat tests on the creature's blood, hoping to find something they had missed earlier. It was a slim hope and proved fruitless. He studied the printout of the results each night, standing in his office and sighing. The blood was *bland*; broken down to its basic genes, it showed a strange mix of reptile and mammal genes, but had the same markers as thousands of other samples from animals already known to science. There was nothing unusual, no obvious genetic differences that might point to cures for diseases or ageing, no oddities that could be exploited to make new medicines or other health treatments. It was just blood. The creature's saliva (and how hard had *that* been to get? Christ, never again!) was the same. No enzymes they didn't already know about, no venom or interesting chemical content, *nothing*. It might be new to science, but in terms of their research, it was boring.

And lethal. The deaths in the field and during the transportation phase might be understandable, but back here? They shouldn't have happened, wouldn't have happened if they had been better prepared. Morris knew that, just as he knew that Bailey's death was his fault and that it should have been him torn to pieces instead of his assistant. He had constantly underestimated the creature, however, simply never thought that it might be anything other than a throwback. Morris had bitter memories of laughing about it on the journey out at the beginning of the expedition, calling it a "lucky survivor" and everyone laughing with him without ever once stopping to ask the questions, How has it been lucky? *Is* it lucky, or are there other reasons for its survival?

Poor Bailey, the only one who ever seemed to have any success in understanding or analysing the creature, was torn to pieces, to *shreds,* as Morris watched. It could disguise itself, that was the problem, in even the barest of terrains. It was doing it now; as Morris looked out of his office and down into the creature's enclosure, he should have been able to see it. It was too large to completely conceal itself in theory, although the rocky outcrop they had built against the far wall did allow it some cover, yet somehow it managed to lose itself in a space slightly less than a thousand square metres. How? How could it do it? It was large, should be easily visible from the vantage point of his office, but no. *Nothing.* It was almost as though it had the skills to make itself invisible, to fade away to near-nothing when it wanted to, reappearing only when it was too late to do anything about it.

Bailey had been in there with guards, all armed, and yet none of them had been able to protect him from the creature as it reared up just next to him and opened its mouth and roared. Morris had screamed and then there was just blood, spraying and fanning as the creature dragged the poor bastard into a dance that whirled towards the entrance and left pieces of Bailey scattered in its wake. Later, when they talked to the guards, none of them remembered seeing or hearing the thing until it rose up in the middle of the protective ring they had supposedly formed about the scientist. Two of them, at *least* two of them, must have practically walked over the fucking thing, but no one saw a thing. Poor Bailey, killed on a mission to collect shit so that they could look for stomach microbes and digestive enzymes. Killed on Morris' mission, because Morris didn't like going into the enclosure and Bailey was always eager to help.

They had managed to get some parts of Bailey back; two larger pieces had been dragged from the drinking pool where they had been washed clean, and some had been found impaled on one of the smaller rock outcrops, grey-pink loops of intestine hanging down below it like ribbons festooning a party-goer's chair. More had been found in the stools collected during the following week's shit run. It wasn't much, Morris reflected, after a life of study, to be found in pieces and half-dissolved in semi-liquid, foul-smelling piles of excrement. Not much at all.

In spite of the lack of progress, Morris worked harder than ever. He pored over test results, staying after everyone but the maintenance staff had left, watching and re-watching film of the creature's behaviour, checking endocrinology and toxicity and blood type and dentition against known species but to no avail. He reread Bailey's notes, hoping to find in them some missed thing, but no. There was nothing. Fucking *nothing*. The creature was large, fast, smart, lithe, cunning, incredibly aggressive and also apparently no more unusual than a vole or a lemur or a fucking *gecko*. It was a survivor from an age that was long gone, they thought, perfectly adapted to a world that did not know it existed. It had given no clues up to them, revealed no secrets to them, showed them nothing other than how to die bloody deaths.

It showed no potential for making money.

On the morning of the fifth day after the Executioner's Visit (as Morris had taken to calling it), he was sitting at his desk when his office darkened. Irritated, he looked around; power outages had happened before, and the office lights and kitchen areas were deemed the most expendable and so first to be sacrificed in the underground facility. His lights were still on, however. He looked towards the window. Most of his office light came in from there, from the daylight-replicating bulbs strung across its enclosure's ceiling. They came on in patterns designed to replicate the creature's normal day and night environment and it should still be a daylight period, he knew. What fresh mess was this?

The creature was clinging to the frame and peering in at him.

Morris couldn't scream. He kicked out, trying to push his chair back, but it rolled scant inches before bumping up against the desk. He heard the click of his teeth as they came together hard and felt his stomach do a cold, queasy roll. It was outside his fucking *window*! It wasn't supposed to be able to get that high, the wall below it was featureless, yet there it was. It seemed vast, a dark shadow blocking the light and coating his office in darkness. One of its arms was stretched out, the heavy claws dragging across the surface of a toughened glass pane that now seemed far too thin. Morris couldn't breathe. He watched as the questing arm found something just outside of the glass near the corner of the frame.

No, not near the corner of the frame, but the frame itself. The creature braced, its arm tensing and its belly flat against the glass and then the whole frame shook as it began to tug. Shimmers of light ran across the surface of the glass as it trembled and then Morris found he could scream. It came out of him in a great swoop which seemed to spur the creature on; it shook at the frame more fiercely, making the glass shudder, its body bumping against the pane and its mouth open to reveal jagged teeth. Saliva sprayed against the window, rolling down the vibrating surface in thick strings as Morris screamed again, turning, knocking over his cold coffee and scattering papers off the desk. He scrabbled, his mind black and empty expect for the image of those teeth, those teeth and claws, those *teeth* and then he found the alarm and pressed it with a finger that felt fat and clumsy and the electric whoop filled the air and drowned his scream and his bladder was letting go because the window was cracking. He heard it, a sharp snapping sound that cut through even the alarm's shrieks and he turned back to the window to see lines snaking through the glass, reaching down from the corner and rooting against the bottom of the frame and fracturing his view of the creature and he screamed again as chunks of glass started to fall away and he could smell it, smell earth and musk and sand and shit and meat and piss, and hear its grunted exhalations like the huffing of some vast laughing god and then it dropped away and Morris collapsed to his knees.

The electric whoop of the alarm still ripped at the air. Morris heard, under it, the distant sound of shouts and then a scream. Slowly, feeling his wet trousers cling and rub at him, he rose and walked to his broken window. Humid air drifted in around him as he looked down into the enclosure and smelled the dense scent of the creature again. It was in the centre of the small grassed plain they had created for it, hunched over and thrashing violently back and forth. A spray of something dark that was probably blood fanned out from below it. Morris heard another scream and something rolled out from under the creature, tumbling down to the edge of the pool. Even from this distance, Morris knew it was a severed head. He could see its hair, matted with blood, and thought he could make out eyes glaring at him.

Beyond the creature, what remained of the security team was regrouping. Morris made out another dark bundle on the ground that left streaks behind it as two of the men dragged it away. There were distant shouts and the phone on Morris' desk began to ring, its shrillness adding to the cacophony. He carried on watching, feeling numb. The creature finished with the man and darted forward, towards the cluster of men further up the slope. They scattered before it, running, but it ignored them. It took a second for Morris to see it; in the chaos, the entry door to the enclosure had been left open.

The numbness went, vanished under a wave of fear that made Morris' belly clench. He shouted, but his voice had no chance against the shriek of the alarm. He ran to his desk, picking up his phone and gabbing into it. Whoever was at the other end tried to talk but he shouted them down.

"Shut the fuck up! Shut up! Shut the door, the enclosure door, it'll get out. It'll get out!" There was a muffled cry from the other end of the line and then silence. Morris dashed back to the window. For the first time since his initial sighting of it all those months ago, before the panic and confusion, he was glad to see the creature; at least it was still in the enclosure. It had one of the security men in a savage embrace, tearing at him. It wasn't far from the door, and the poor bastard had probably got in its way. Its head was slick with gore, glittering and demonic in the fake sunlight, and then the doors began to close.

The effect on the creature was immediate; it dropped the man, spattering his remains behind it as it darted towards the door and thrust his head into the narrowing exit, its broad shoulders crashing against the steel panels. The gears howled as they tried to force the doors closed, the creature writhing and thrashing against them. Its claws clattered furiously against the metal as it scrabbled, its head swinging back and forth. It was hissing, Morris heard, a hollow sound of fury audible even over the alarm. The door mechanism crashed again and the creature finally jerked its head free, the doors swinging shut with a boom. Morris' phone rang again. He picked it up without taking his eyes off the creature, which was throwing itself at the doors and roaring.

"There are men in there!" shouted whoever was at the other end of the line.

"Leave them," said Morris. "They'll keep it occupied while we sort this fucking mess out. I need the window in my office sealed, it's not going to be long before it remembers and tries to get out here."

"The men . . . " said whoever, before their voice trailed off into nothing.

"I said to leave them. And turn the fucking alarm off."

The alarm clattered into silence with a dying electronic wail as Morris watched the creature back away from the door. At the far end of the enclosure, the security team were gathered at the base of the rocks, clumped together. They were shouting, and one was waving at Morris, holding the gas rifle in his hand. Morris wondered briefly if the team had managed to fire off any shots before everything turned to shit, or whether the drugs in the darts simply weren't good enough to tranquilise the creature. He raised a hand to the man, a gesture of sympathy and sorrow, but then dropped it again. Below him, the creature was stalking towards the men, and Morris had to turn away.

"How many?"

"Nine in all."

"And still it has provided us with nothing? Your retests have showed up nothing of interest?"

"Nothing."

"Doctor Morris, this is unacceptable. It is costing us money. Serious money."

"Yes. I'm sorry."

"I'm sure. The project is terminated, Doctor Morris. Please implement what is no longer the least desirable solution, but has become a necessity. The board wants the thing dead by the end of the day. We might still be able to obtain something useful from it after a full dissection. It is clear to us now that this should have been our first action upon obtaining the creature."

"Yes."

"And Doctor Morris?"

"Yes?"

"Be ready to explain yourself in full at the next board meeting."

Morris' window had been replaced by a thick steel sheet whose welding marks were keloid and wormlike in their thickness. The sheet made his office much darker but it didn't matter, he knew that now. He wouldn't be here much longer; none of them would. Underneath the facility's more usual background noise was a new sound, that of air pumps. A powerful poison was being pumped in to the creature's enclosure, and soon the damned thing would be dead. And good riddance, Morris thought, good bloody riddance. This was supposed to have been his big chance, an opportunity to prove himself but instead it had turned into a disaster. He would be forever associated with the deaths of everyone the creature had killed, would always be known as the man who failed in his job. Morris hated the creature, was frightened of it, felt helpless in the face of the implacable impossibility of understanding it or controlling it, and he was glad that, finally, it was being killed.

Morris could see it now on the screen on his desk, hastily installed to replace the view of the enclosure lost when the window was sealed. It was by the pool, struggling to breathe, its chest rising and falling jerkily. Good. Let it suffer. It had slaughtered the entire security team, killed Morris' colleagues, destroyed his career. Let that *fucking* creature die a painful, slow death.

It was going into spasm now, dark liquid spraying from its mouth and anus, slathering across the sand. It lowered its head and drank but immediately vomited, spraying water that was now tinged a rusty pink back into the pool. Morris grinned, then laughed. The creature tried to drink again, vomited again; raised its head to stretch its neck, opened its mouth, retched without producing anything. Collapsed. Was it dead? No, it was still breathing, its inhalations and exhalations birdlike. Exultant, Morris carried on watching. It was in the final throes now, and soon it would be gone.

The enclosure stank, a sour smell like meat that had been exposed to the sun for too long. Morris and the removal team approached the dead creature cautiously, moving around the patches of bloody vomit and watery shit that dotted the enclosure floor. The creature had taken several more hours to die, surprising Morris with its tenacity. He shouldn't have been surprised; nothing about this damn thing should have surprised him now, but even so, it had proved impressively hardy. It had staggered its way around the enclosure, slowing to a crawl before finally coming to rest splayed out on its back at the point where the scrub gave way to slightly longer grasses. It hadn't moved in hours, it belly exposed and its legs limp.

It was dead.

The team rolled the huge stretcher across to the creature and started to prepare the strapping. Morris walked close to it and took one last look at the thing before it became the responsibility of others. It was hideous, huge and dark and primal. Its claws, still caked with a scurf of dried blood, glittered and its fangs appeared huge. Morris leaned in close, whispering "Fuck you," to it. He wanted to spit on it but dared not in case the men saw. He still had some reputation left and he needed to protect it. Instead, he consoled himself with another whispered "Fuck you". Morris stared at the creature. One eye, the pupil dark and the inner eyelid half-down, stared at Morris. It still retained the moisture of life, glistening, reflecting the shadows of the men that moved about it, the dark orb glacial and rolling.

Blinking.

It happened fast. The creature flipped itself over, landing, finding its footing and streaking towards the men in one blinding movement. The first man fell beneath its claws without having a chance to scream, but Morris was screaming, screaming and running as the rest of the team scattered. From the corner of his eye, he saw the creature leap over the stretcher and onto a woman he thought might have been called Mary and then a *fleur-de-lis* of blood was spraying from where her throat had been and Morris was running faster. The entrance to the enclosure gaped at him from across the sloping ground, its dark maw inviting and yet oh so far away, and he ran and ran and ran.

Morris heard a scream from behind him, heard a roar like the shifting of tectonic plates, heard the ineffectual whoop of redundant alarms, smelled an aroma of musk and wildness and then the creature was at his side. It paced him and then shifted away and another of the team was down and screaming and dying. Morris shrieked, feeling his muscles spasm as the creature reappeared in his peripheral vision. Another of the team ran past him, faster, younger and kicking his legs high to stay moving on the damp earth. For a moment, the man (*Marlowe*, Morris thought, *Marlowe*) was between Morris and the creature and then a dark shape rose up behind him and dropped, its arms outstretched. Marlowe managed to let loose a wild cry which was choked off as the creature clamped its jaws around his head and then a great fern of blood was blooming from Marlowe and licking against Morris' skin as he pushed himself and ran faster.

The heavy grasses tore at Morris' legs as he reached the top of the low slope. The rock formation loomed to his side, the blank wall of the enclosure ahead of him, the creature behind him. Behind? No, to his other side, racing across the sand and grass and *oh Christ it was coming it was coming!* blood streaming from its mouth and roaring with a sound like reality tearing and its eyes black as death. Morris ran, hearing the pounding of the thing behind him and then he was through the enclosure doorway and into the corridor. Here, the sound of the alarms was almost unbearable, echoing and harsh in the narrow concrete tunnels, but loud as they were they could not drown out the sound of the creature's approach. It claws skittered on the hard floor and its breath panted around Morris' shoulders. He saw another door ahead of him, heard the sound of the creature banging and scraping against the walls as it ran after him, saw the door get closer and closer as his legs pumped and his lungs shrieked and then he smacked into the door and oh thank *fuck* it opened and he was through.

It was an office. Morris slammed the door shut just as the creature hit against it, making the heavy wood shiver in the frame. Morris cried, backing away and feeling for something he could use, some weapon. There was a desk covered in paper, a laptop, a set of shelves on the wall full of books. Morris saw a photo in a frame of a pretty blonde woman standing by a statue of a naked man, but no weapons. He heard another scream and a roar and something breaking and then the door shook violently again. The wood splintered, the top panel cracking and folding to reveal the creature's bullet head. Morris heard a scream and realised it was coming from him because the door was cracking down its centre as the creature pushed against it, its roar filling the office. Morris backed around the desk as the creature pressed further into the room. He picked up something, a mug, and threw it, watched it bounce off the monstrous snout without effect. The creature hissed, spitting saliva across the desk and Morris' face, warm greasy strings that stank. Thrashing, it forced its way further in and Morris, backed up against the wall, saw hope lost in its depthless eyes and gaping mouth.

And then it was gone.

Something in the corridor crashed and the creature snarled, snapping back out of the doorway and darting away. Morris heard more screams, the sound of things breaking or being broken, the alarms whooping, his own breath ragged in his chest. He was still alive! *Oh, thank God!* He collapsed forwards, falling against the desk and weeping. He heard a distant screech, furious and animal, and the sound of glass shattering. He remained still, leaning on the desk until his legs felt strong enough to support him. The sounds of destruction grew more distant as the creature moved through the facility. Morris sniffed; below the powerful stench of the creature, he smelled burning plastic. *Christ, what a fuckup.* He'd get the blame for this, he knew, but how could he have known? The fucking thing had played *dead,* for God's sake. And besides, the poison should have killed it, not just made it ill. How much damage had it done? How many dead were there, all ready to lie at Morris' feet? He let out a helpless moan; everything was fucked. He was fucked.

Eventually Morris went to the door and peered into the corridor. The emergency lights flashed orange, created moving shadows, but other than that it was deserted. The alarms shrieked on, not quite drowning the chaotic sounds from another part of the facility. Morris tried to work out where it was coming from; somewhere towards the canteen, he thought. He heard the sound of something metal being scattered (tables? chairs?) and another roar. Someone shouted *"Oh Jesus no!"* and screamed and Morris knew he had to move.

He went as fast as he could along the corridor, staying silent. He came to the intersection and turned right, away from the creature which was to his left and deeper inside the complex. The sounds of it were clearer here, grunts and hissing and snarls and the sound of its claws clattering across the floor. Morris' distant colleagues moaned and screamed, a terrible punctuation to what was happening. The air was hazy with acrid smoke, hanging in lazy sheets that coiled and swirled around his head. If he could get out, he realised, he could seal the facility and simply let it burn, let the flames kill the bastard thing.

The entrance was five nightmarish minutes away. Morris saw no one else on his journey, although he heard someone shouting that they should come on, *come on* at one point. The air was thickening with smoke, making it hard to breathe. He spat, hoping to clear his throat, but his sputum felt dry and rough in his mouth. Behind him, the noise of the creature seemed louder. Was it getting closer? Coming this way, following its prey, all of them herding towards the exit? Morris had to get there first, avoid the crowds. If he could stay ahead of the others, they might distract the creature, letting him get out. He ran faster, all pretence at silence forgotten.

He was there! The entrance stood ahead of him, and he began to cry as he ran towards it. The heavy doors were open and through them he saw the night; the day had ended whilst he had been in the facility. For one glorious moment, he thought he was going to make it and then something heavy hit his back and he was on the floor.

The creature stood above him, saliva and blood slicked across its face. Its mouth was open, its teeth gleaming a pale ivory in the artificial light. It almost looked as though it were grinning and Morris screamed and tried to crawl away, feeling the flesh of his back move against itself in a way that was both unnatural and agonising. He saw blood on the floor and wondered if it was his and thought it probably was; saw the creature's shadow eclipse the blood and felt it dip its head in close.

Morris screamed again. It was a loud scream, desperate and lost. It only lasted for a moment.

The creature sniffed at the air, tasting the new scents and enjoying its new freedom. Behind it, the alarms wailed but no one came; it had eaten well, but was still hungry. It shook itself, sending droplets of blood dancing into the night sky. It sniffed again, smelling food nearby. Slowly at first but gathering speed as it went, it loped away, towards the lights of the nearby village and the town beyond.

TRAFFIC STREAM

"**A**L? I'M REALLY sorry, but I'm running late. Are you okay to wait for me?"

Bird sighed inwardly. It had been a long day, and this was already going to be a late meeting; Samuels was only passing through, he said, but wanted to see Bird if he could wait until oh, maybe half past six? Samuels was one of Bird's best customers, and now he was running late, which meant Bird would run late as well.

"No problem," said Bird. "When do you think you might be here?"

"I don't know," said Samuels. "I'm still on the main road, and the traffic's bad. Even the side roads look busy. Has there been an accident?"

He was still on the main road, which meant Bird had at least fifteen more minutes to wait, probably more. Bird looked out of his office window at the dark winter sky and the quiet roads of the industrial estate. "Not that I know of," he said. "There's no traffic here and normally we get backed up if something's happened on the roads. It's probably just the end of rush hour." Samuels disconnected the call as Bird continued looking out of the window, gazing at the world outside his office. Past the network of roads and buildings of the industrial estate that housed his company, he could see glimpses of the main route that passed alongside the estate and which fed it. Lights glimmered as they rushed along it; it was busy, but not unusually so. *All of my staff are in that*, he thought. *All of them, in it or already through it and home, all of them except me.* Bird tried not to be too irritated; a good meeting with Samuels could secure a significant chunk of their income for the forthcoming months and besides, time in the quiet office gave him chance to catch up on his paperwork. Sighing, this time out loud, he went back to his filing.

"Al, it's me again. I've got myself completely lost, I'm afraid. My satnav has sent me off on a side road and now it's playing up, won't tell me where I am and I don't recognise anything, so I'm going to have to turn back until I get to the main road and then try to work it out from there." Behind Samuels' voice Bird could hear traffic humming, the heavy wash of lorries and the lighter, more insistent *swish* of cars, a discordant soundtrack to the fragile connection between the two men. He looked at his clock, annoyed and hoping that his irritation wouldn't show in his voice. It was already gone seven and at this rate, Samuels wouldn't be here for another half-hour. Bird's hopes of spending some relaxing time at home before bed were being gradually submerged, diluted away. He stood, carrying the phone over to the window.

"What do you mean, the satnav sent you down the wrong road?"

"It told me to turn," said Samuels, "but there were two roads off the main road next to each other, and it didn't say which one. I took the first and as soon as I was on it, the satnav told me we were on the wrong road, that it was recalculating the route but then it made a gurgling noise and crapped out on me and it hasn't shown a sign of life since. This is the wrong road, though."

"Wrong?"

"I've been to you before, and I remember that the whole way there I was always surrounded by buildings, but now I've gone wrong. I'm hopeless without the satnav, and now its sent me wrong and I'm in the middle of nowhere. It's funny, I didn't travel far down this road, just until I could pull over and ring you, but it's like I've driven to another country. I'm surrounded by fields."

"Farmland?" asked Bird, thinking that the only farm he knew of was about ten miles away, and that Samuels must be badly off-track if he was there.

"No, it's not farmland. Actually, even 'fields' isn't quite right. There's open ground, but there's lots of trees and bushes or hedges and the ground looks to be mud rather than grass...and there's lots other plants I don't recognise. The ground's not very even, there are tracks and roads all over the place. There's quite a lot of cars about still. Any idea where I am?"

"No," replied Bird. It didn't sound like anywhere he knew.

"Oh well. It's pretty busy so hopefully it shouldn't be hard to get back on the right road."

"Okay," said Bird. "I'll see you when you get here."

"Shall we postpone 'till next I'm up this way? I know this must be inconveniencing you. You have a family, don't you?"

"A wife and son," said Bird shortly. The offer was there, all he had to do was accept but he couldn't because, honestly, he didn't think it was a real offer. It was made for him to turn down, to show that Samuels was a cause to accept inconvenience for, to prove just how big a fish he was in Bird's little pond. "No," said Bird, "still come."

—.—

"I'm still lost," said Samuels. "I couldn't find anywhere to turn around to get back to the main carriageway, so I carried on hoping to see a sign or come to a roundabout, but there's nothing out here. I tried one of the little side roads in the hope it'd bring me round but it's not and now I have no idea where I am."

"Tell me what you can see, perhaps I can help," said Bird. His paperwork was done, he had got ahead of himself by preparing for the next day's meetings and he had spent the previous half-hour leafing through a newspaper he had found in the secretaries' office. He had managed a few words with Christopher before his son went to bed, although Patty hadn't allowed him long. She had been distinctly frosty with him and he could only hope that Samuels would get here soon, and that they would be finished quickly, so that he could get home and apologise in person whilst she was still awake. His office was large and airless yet felt curiously claustrophobic.

"More of the mud and trees and bushes," Samuels said, "and lots of those other plants as well. They look like yucca, palms, or cactuses or something."

"Cacti?" asked Bird. "We're in the north of England, the cactus isn't common around here." Actually, it was unheard of. Perhaps the darkness was confusing Samuels.

"I didn't say they were cacti, only that they looked like them," said Samuels, his voice toneless yet somehow defensive. "There's all sorts, in amongst the trees and bushes. Some are small, some are tall, but they're all funny shapes, sticking up. I can't see them properly, but they're all sorts of colours and they're swaying in the wind."

Bird looked out of his window again. The night was silent, the sparse and bony trees that lined the car park motionless.

Looking up, the clouds clinging to the underside of the sky also hung, fragile and still.

"There's a lot of cars about," said Samuels. "There's roads everywhere, most full of traffic, but there's no streetlights so it's dark except for the headlights, hard to see. I've pulled over again to try and get my bearings. Of all the times for the damn satnav to break down!" He laughed, but it didn't sound genuine. "Any ideas?"

"Can you see any buildings? Or bigger roads?" asked Bird. He couldn't think of anywhere like the place Samuels was describing, but in truth he didn't know this area particularly well; he simply passed through it morning and night, coming in to the office or returning home and he rarely looked at anything other than the ribbon of road ahead of him as he travelled.

"No. There's just headlights, although most of them seem to be going one way, towards something. Could it be you?"

"I doubt it," replied Bird. "Most of the units here are closed for the night, although there might be some on the other side of the park still open. I know there's a distribution warehouse that sometimes works through the night, maybe it's them. Anyway, follow them and we'll see where you get to."

"Okay, I will do and JESUS *CHRIST*!" Samuels suddenly screamed, his voice distorting and rising to a screech, making Bird yank the phone away from his ear. Even with it at arm's length, he could hear Samuels shouting "You stupid bastards!"

"What's wrong? Are you okay?" asked Bird, bringing the phone close to his ear again.

"Jesus!" said Samuels. "Three idiots came barrelling along way too fast, and right behind them was a big damned truck going just as fast, maybe even faster. It scared the crap out of me, they came so close that my car rocked. Jesus. God knows what speed they were going." He let out a breath that hitched down in steps as it travelled from Samuels' phone to Bird's.

"I know this is turning into a late night, and I'm sorry Al," said Samuels, his voice soft in the electronic sea, "but I'd really appreciate it if you'd wait for me. I could do with a coffee and to see a friendly face before I do much more driving."

"No problem," said Bird again, and meant it. Samuels sounded weary, and he suddenly felt sorry for the man. Driving wasn't a favourite thing of his, and to do the miles that Samuels must have to do would surely be a lonely and tense experience. "Drive safe and I'll see you soon."

At three minutes past eight Bird's phone rang out and even before he answered it, he knew who it would be and what he would say. "I'm still lost," said Samuels apologetically. "I've had to pull over again to call you. The way these idiots are driving, it's a miracle I've not been hit by one of them. I mean, everyone's driving like lunatics. It's getting really dark now and I don't seem to be able to get any closer to you. Most of the cars and lorries still seem to be heading along the road in one direction, though, so if I follow them, I should find my way to you."

"Can you see a company name on the lorries?" asked Bird.

"Funny thing, but no. Everything's going so fast it's impossible to see them properly, there's no light except their headlights. The cars are the same, just little blurs swimming along the road, all of them going so fast it's frightening. They must all be going somewhere, though, so I'm hoping if I follow this road, it'll either come to you, or at least back to the main road."

The main carriageway that flowed through the industrial estate was quiet; Bird could see it from his window and should have been able to see anything heading along it towards or from the distribution warehouse. Nothing moved along its length, not car or truck or lorry or even watchman's bike or stray dog. So where were all the vehicles Samuels could see coming from? Or going to? Where was he?

"I'm no closer." It was ten minutes later and now Samuels sounded angry and anxious. "I can't believe how much traffic there is, but I seem to be going in circles. I follow someone but they turn left and right and left again, and they're going so fast and they're dangerous, too. I was following a string of cars along the road and one of the lorries came out in front of me from off a sidestreet I hadn't even seen because there are no lights, and I swear it didn't look, just came out and started after the cars. Christ, it was so close, how it missed me I don't know. The cars sped up, and I lost them. I mean, I tried to follow them, but I couldn't keep up. Didn't want to really, they were going too damned quick. I've tried to follow a couple of lorries as well, but I either can't keep up or I end up back where I started from. At least, I think it's where I started from, I can't tell because there's no light and everything looks the same. Where am I, Al?"

"I don't know," said Bird. "If I give you my mobile number, could you try to take a photograph of one of the trucks and send it to me? I might recognise it, be able to work out where it's from. If I can do that, I might be able to work out where they're headed. There may be a depot round here that I don't know about and if there is, I might be able to figure out where you are. Tell me what you can see. Is there anything unusual?"

"You mean besides cars and lorries driving like morons, like they're chasing each other? No," said Samuels. "There are just trees and those other plants and weird hills like dunes and valleys between them and streets all around, and cars and trucks going around and around. There are no lights still, no streetlights or building lights, nothing, just headlights." He fell silent apart from his breathing, echoing and hollow in Bird's ear. Then, with a sound almost like he was shaking himself like a dog shaking water from its fur, Samuels said, "I'll try to take a photograph and send it you. Give me your number."

The picture arrived five minutes later. Samuels had taken it from in front and to the side of the truck as it raced by, his camera flat so that the picture was landscape rather than portrait. At the right side of the screen was the dazzle of one headlight, high and glittering and above it a cab that seemed smooth and metallic and receding, its colour lost to the surrounding darkness. Below the light was a wide, blurred suggestion of a grille and under it, a sweep of darkness broken by a grey patch that might have been a wheel but that seemed too thin to support the vehicle above. Dropping away from the cab and taking up the rest of the picture was the lorry's body, but its side was either plain or the words were, like the top of the cab, lost to the darkness. The only details that Bird could make out along the body was a peculiar, elongated lateral ridge shaped like the edge of a jutting coin partway along, where the lorry's canvas wall had (he assumed) rippled out because of the speed that it was travelling. The only light in the picture was the headlight, although the side of the truck glittered slightly as though its material wall was metallic. Bird peered at the image, trying to discern some familiar detail from it. A moment later, his phone rang.

"Well?"

"I'm sorry, I don't recognise it," said Bird. "I've checked the directory we have here as well, and there's only the one distribution warehouse on the estate. I rang them a moment ago and they're shut, so wherever those lorries are heading, it's not here."

"They're not heading anywhere."

"Pardon?" said Bird; he had heard Samuels clearly enough, but what he said made no sense. The other man's voice was dreamy somehow, flat and distant and subdued.

"They aren't going anywhere, at least, not one place. They're going up and down the roads and streets, both directions. There's hundreds of them, cars and trucks. Some of the trucks are huge, others are smaller. Some have lots of headlights, so many that they're dazzling. Some of them have only got two. None of them have rear lights."

"None of them?" asked Bird, going yet again to the window. Even the road outside the industrial estate, what little of it he could see, was quiet now, and he wondered if Samuels was having some kind of breakdown.

"None," confirmed Samuels. "Just front lights. The cars are the most beautiful colours, by the way. I see them as they go past. Bright reds and blues and greens and purples and silvers, not just one colour but lots. Beautiful."

He's gone mad, thought Bird, but he kept the thought to himself and instead said, "Can you see any buildings yet?"

"Some of the lorries, trucks, whatever they are haven't got lights at all," said Samuels, apparently ignoring Bird. "I just saw one come on to the road from over the mud. Right over the top of the slope, down onto the road and in behind some of these little cars." He paused, and in the space between the conversation Bird heard the frantic, tidal noise of vehicles hurtling past Samuels. "The air's funny too, heavier than it should be. When I got out of the car to take the photograph I sent you, I couldn't move very easily, and when something goes past me, the car rocks for longer than it should. What's happened, Al?"

"I don't know," replied Bird, truthfully. "Are you sure you're okay?" A futile, redundant question; of course Samuels wasn't okay. He was very, very far from okay, far out from shore. Surprisingly, however, Samuels made the head-clearing noise again and when he spoke he sounded clearer, more alert. "No, I'm fine. I'm going to have to just keep going, I think. I can't apologise enough, Al, but please don't go home yet. I really need a coffee now, and I'm sure I'll find you soon."

"I'm sure you will," said Bird, forcing himself to sound cheerful. "The kettle's on, the coffee's waiting. After all, you can't be far away, can you?"

"No," said Samuels. "I can't be, can I?" And the phone went silent.

When the phone trilled again five minutes later, Bird was almost expecting it. What he wasn't expecting was the shriek that emerged from speaker, tinny and distorted, as he lifted it and connected to the call. Samuels was crying out, a long ululation in which Bird heard no words, only half-formed sounds of fury. As it settled, Samuels voice dropped until Bird made out swearing, loud and fierce and repeated, eventually trailing off into breathless gulps. Through his exhalations, Samuels to Bird, "It nearly got me then!"

"Who did? What's wrong?"

"The lorry! I'm sorry, I'm driving and speaking, shouldn't be I know, but I needed to speak to someone."

"About what?" said Bird, beginning to lose his temper. Mad or not, lost or not, it was late and Bird was emphatically in Patty's bad books and Samuels was, good customer or not, becoming an annoyance.

"The lorries, the cars. I just saw one! It ate the car, fucking ate it!"

Bird didn't reply immediately, and in the pause in the

conversation he heard the sound of Samuel's engine, full-throated and straining. "How fast are you going?" he asked.

"It came up behind one of the little cars and then, I don't know, it opened somehow and the car was gone," said Samuels, his voice loud, hysteria audible and strident in its tone. "No wonder the cars are going so fast, the lorries, trucks, whatever the fuck they are, they're chasing them. Everywhere I look, they're chasing them, round the roads and streets, cutting across the hills, going between the trees. There are cars hiding behind the plants and trees, you know. Did you know?"

"No," said Bird, thinking, *Poor sod. He's gone.*

"I saw them before I had to start driving fast, just drifting behind the plants and keeping away from the roads until the lorries see them and then they're off, fast as they can go! What? Oh, *FUCK*!"

"Samuels? Samuels?" said Bird, but the connection was gone, the phone swimming in dead air. Bird dialled Samuels' number but the call was redirected to the voicemail service. He left a message for Samuels to ring him as soon as he could, and then set his phone down on his desk. Moments later, it rang and he snatched it up.

"Samuels?"

"Jesus, it nearly got me then. One of the little trucks came out from behind the trees and tried to catch me, but I was too quick!"

"Samuels, where are you?"

"Fuck knows. It's right behind me, but I'm fast. Jesus, it's close, *Jesus*. Fuck him, though, fuck him. I'm not letting it catch me, no. I can see bits of cars stuck to its front. Bits of the cars, all over its front and pieces by the roads, but it's not getting me." Samuels paused and Bird heard the sound of his engine and the deep rip of something else, something close, the sound coruscating and wet, and then Samuels was talking again.

"I'm fast, I'm fast, I can outrun it. I—" and the phone went silent once more. Bird let out a frustrated snarl and dialled Samuels' number, but this time the phone simply refused to connect him. He tried several more times, getting the same result each time. He stopped and, after a moment's thought, not knowing if he was doing the right thing or not, he called the police. It was late and he was tired, worried about Samuels and the other drivers he might encounter. As he waited to be connected to the local traffic office, he pulled his mobile from his pocket and called up the picture Samuels had sent him. With the darkness pressing against his window like the depths of some vast ocean, he studied the image again, hoping he might see something in it that he had missed before. It was as blurred and unclear as the last time he looked at it, but he couldn't help but think about what Samuels had said in his last calls, about the sound of his voice and the wet, loud sounds that had darted in the background. Now, the grille of the lorry looked like a gaping mouth, full of curved and beckoning teeth.

A MAN OF ICE AND SORROW

MAINS WALKED MILES every day. Behind his home, the land started to rise, buckling as it went and forming itself into hills and valleys covered by a dislocating green jumble of trees. It was hard terrain, made worse by the bleak weather; the ground sweated ice and frost and, most days or nights, the snow fell in fat, greasy flakes that lay on the ground in drifts. If he walked in the morning, the crust of the snow was frozen and cracked under his feet with a sound like tiny bones breaking. If he walked later in the day it softened, and would cling to his legs and feet in heavy clumps. On days when the wind dropped to nothing, the falling snow damped the sound out of the world so that he walked in a featureless, oppressive silence. It should have been easy to get lost in the dense and sprawling tangle of trees, but Mains hadn't managed that trick yet, no matter how hard he tried; every day, he found his way home.

The day he came across the first snowman, Mains was up early. He had had another bad night, with sleep capering most of the time just out of his reach, and he set out not long after sunrise. His boots kicked their way through the new

snow, brittle with cold, as he walked across the open land
and to the lower edge of the hillside's tree cover. His skin
tightened under his beard, pulling taut over his cheekbones
as the frigid air nipped at him, and his nose ran steadily.
Under the cover of the trees, the air filled with sounds—the
frayed whistle of a breeze broken by branches and trunks,
the loose patter of flakes and ice falling from branches, his
own breath straining in and out of his lungs. He walked fast,
following no path but simply rising with the contours of the
hill, threading a random path between the glowering trunks
and over ridges of clasping roots.

The snowman was standing at the upper edges of the trees,
perhaps fifty yards beyond the treeline but facing down the
slope, so that it appeared to be watching Mains as he
emerged from between two trunks. It caught Mains, who
tended to walk with his head down, by surprise; he glimpsed
a figure ahead of him, unexpected and motionless, and he
started slightly before realising what it was that stared at him.
His heart rate, which had spiked sharply with the shock,
jittered down to its previous rate as he went to the snowman
and looked it over, wonderingly.

It was near-perfect, a bulbous thing like a cartoonist's
version of an ideal snowman. It had a large spherical base
mounted by a smaller sphere for the lower and upper body,
and a smaller sphere than that for its head. Whoever had
built the snowman had managed to find branches to form its
arms, thin and black and split at their ends into smaller twigs
like fingers, and had set them so they curved forward,
attempting to embrace whoever came close. A line of stones
had been set into the snowman's cheerful, rounded belly to
form buttons, and a scrap of something (a bag from the local
supermarket, Mains thought) had been wrapped around the
junction between the body and the head; the bright colours

were jaunty against its white flesh. It had an old cap upon its head, tilted back and at a rakish angle.

The only fault with the snowman that Mains could find was the face under the cap, which was oddly constructed. The nose made of a carrot was as expected, but the mouth below, made of smaller stones, was turned down into a grimace. The coal-chip eyes were shiny, but tilted out so that the overall expression was one of confusion or misery, an impression compounded by the furrows like frown-lines that were etched into its forehead and deepened by the shadows that gathered below the carefully sculpted ridges of snow. It had stones set into the side of its head, like ears, big and sticking out and it made Mains smile and then laugh to see it, even as he pondered the skill involved in making it. He took his phone from his pocket and took several photos of the snowman, grinning; Johnny would love this, would laugh in childish glee at the jolly, rotund figure.

And then he remembered. Johnny wouldn't love the pictures of the snowman, wouldn't laugh at the cap that looked like one of Mains' old ones or the ears that stuck out from its head, because Johnny was dead.

In the aftermath of the accident, when Mains' shattered leg bones were quietly starting to knit back together and the metal cage surrounding his knee often hummed and vibrated and jolted against the anchorages in his flesh, Mains and Elise had tried hard; they had, he was sure of that. Around their bitterness and mourning and a pain that felt to Mains like constant razor slashes under his skin, they had tried as hard as they could not to fall apart. They had made the arrangements for Johnny's funeral, choosing songs he liked and readings that meant something to them, burying him in the churchyard that contained all of Elise's deceased family for the previous three generations. After, when he was used to the wheelchair, Mains tried to return to work, as did Elise, and they both attended his occupational therapy appointments. Elise nagged him gently when he tried to get out of his exercises at home, and praised him when he started to walk again. They saw friends and family, accepted condolences as best they could, only crying when they were alone together. Ultimately, however, it wasn't enough.

Back in his cottage, Mains ate because he had to, chewing his food to a paste as tasteless as wet cardboard. His leg ached and he spent a long time in the bath that night, not looking at the thick keloid scarring that traced its way around his knee and across his thigh. It was too easy to look at the scars and remember, to feel the thin carapace of his coping begin to crack under the memories. After bathing, he watched television for an hour but the images that moved across the screen were pointless and flat and so he turned the set off and sat in the dark. There seemed little point in turning the light on; even if he wanted to, he knew he wouldn't be able to read. When he went to bed, he lay awake for hours thinking about the snowman, about how Johnny would have laughed with delight at it, and he only realised he was crying when he heard himself sob and felt the cold tears trickle down his cheeks.

Mains must eventually have slept, for he woke late the next morning, feeling as though the air itself was pressing down on him, heavy on his shoulders. Heavier than normal. He had missed a call as he slept, Elise leaving one of her short, businesslike messages about some element of their finances that hadn't been sorted, that still tied them together like damp, knotted string. As he dressed, Mains tried to think about the contents of her message, but found that it had already slipped away from him. The insurance payout, negotiated on their behalf by a lawyer friend of his during the period his body healed and they buried their son and tried to find their footing again, had given them both financial security, a bitter irony that wasn't lost on Mains—his son in exchange for a life free from debt. What was left between him and Elise now was the details of their old life, the house that they hadn't yet managed to sell, the few joint items that had some slight emotional meaning for them and that they were trying to be amicable about. That, and the memory of Johnny, bright and gleeful and beautiful and dead at eight.

There was another snowman. Actually, there were several, scattered through the trees at the upper edge of the slope, but all facing upwards. Whoever had made them was skilful, thought Mains as he went around the figures. Here were two, a man and a woman, arms wrapped around each other and smiling; there was a family, the two taller figures clustered protectively around the two smaller ones. The original figure waited, stoic and exposed, beyond the trees.

Why waiting?

It *was* waiting, Mains realised, although for what he had no idea. Standing in amongst the trees alongside the new figures, he looked up at the first snowman. Despite the fresh snowfall overnight, it had kept its shape and definition well and even at a distance, Mains could make out its turned-mouth expression and its curved, beckoning arms. The snow had added musculature to the arms, thickening them to something more than the spindled things they had been the day before, giving them weight and solidity. The snowman looked oddly lost, almost miserable.

Lonely.

Who was making these snowmen and women, wondered Mains. There were no footprints left to show their movements because of the night's snowfall, no telltale tracks of rolled snowballs to make bases and bellies and heads. Nothing. It was a mystery, the first one that had interested him since his life had broken into sharp, fragile pieces. Why here? They were over ten miles from the nearest town, and even the nearest village was perhaps four miles distant; it was one of the reasons he had come here after telling Elise that he couldn't stay married to her.

Was it children? No, the figures were too detailed, too precise. There was patience in their creation as well as skill, patience in the careful etching of features into the snow of the faces and the use of branches and rocks to make expressions and postures. Besides, the figures were, apart from the lone male above the trees, in poses of domesticity and security, and they weren't in a place where they could be easily seen. They seemed built not for any observer but for the builder's own pleasure, the creations not of children but of adults, a person or persons who had taken the time to come out here and build another six figures during the night.

Mains had never been able to truly explain it to Elise. The closest he had ever managed to come was at the end of a night of argument and accusation, after they had fallen quiet in the dying warmth of their marriage bed. "It feels like I'm betraying him," he had said.

"That's silly," Elise had replied. "He'd want you to be as happy as you can. Edward, he'd want *us* to be happy, to be together. He loved us, you know that. We were happiest together, all of us, *together*."

"*Were* happiest, that's the point," said Mains helplessly. There were no words for it, not really, nothing to explain how the feeling of grief had shifted from the sharpest razor slash to a blunt mallet's blow, and even that was fading, slowly but surely. How could he tell her that he was terrified

104

of losing the pain, terrified of losing his grief? Better to keep opening it up, to add more grief on top of it and keep it raw, so that he could keep the memories of his son fresh; better to lose Elise so that he could keep his son. It made little sense, he knew, but that's how it was. That night, Elise had rolled away from him, crying, and he had cried too, silent in the dark, but the next day the tears had gone and they had started the slow process of disentangling.

Mains wasn't going to go to the snowmen the next day, not liking the idea that his daily walks were anything other than random or that he was beginning to find something interesting, but he found that he went to them without thinking. The weather had worsened in the hours that he had slept (again, badly) and the ground beneath even the heaviest cover of trees was bloated with snow, blown in drifts and piled in the hollows and against the trunks like fungus. His leg ached, the bands of muscle above and below the knee trembling as he walked. Snow fell from the branches above him, catching in his eyelashes and along the brim of his cap, making him blink away coarse flakes constantly so that he could see again. *Why am I doing this?* he wondered. *To see snowmen? Because I know Johnny would have liked them? There's lots Johnny would have liked that I don't do, so why this?* As to most of the questions that occurred in his life now, Mains had no answers for himself, so he simply walked on.

There were more figures. Another family group had sprouted in a small clearing, this time the clearly-female adult figure holding a baby whilst the male adult crouched by two older children. How a thing made of spheres, with no legs, could crouch, Mains didn't know, but it was. Its bottom sphere was somehow flattened, elongated, made into the loose image of legs bent at the knees. One figure, distorted and grotesque at a distance, resolved itself into a snow couple, face to face and kissing, pressing together and arms around each other in a proprietorial embrace. There was even a snow dog, sitting at the feet of a snowman that was looking through the trees at a snowwoman, a look on his face of affection and love. The first snowman, the one Mains had begun to think of as his own, was still alone beyond the trees, its face turned to the hill below it.

As Mains opened his cottage door, the telephone was ringing, and it continued for a long time as though challenging him to ignore it. Eventually, he answered.

"Hello, Edward." Elise, her voice distant and polite. "How are you?"

"I'm fine. Well, not fine, but you know."

"No, I don't, Edward. You haven't spoken to me for weeks. I wondered if you'd had chance to think about the message I left you? It's a reasonable offer on the house, and with the markets the way they are, we aren't likely to get a better one. It's a family," her voice softened, thickened. "They have a child. He'll like the garden."

"That's fine, Elise," said Mains. He didn't know what to say. He missed her, he loved her, he wanted her but he couldn't allow himself to tell her and in the silence of his reply, she said 'goodbye' and put the phone down.

When he had first moved here, Elise's calls had been longer, friendly, and apart from his trips to the nearby village for supplies, were just about his only human contact. It was only over time that they changed, became shorter and less personal, and one day he realised with sadness that she had been flirting with him, that the hope of him changing his mind had lain under those early conversations. Over the months, as he refused to be anything other than distant, he heard her close herself off to him, heard anger and then sadness and finally a kind of wintry disappointment came to inhabit her voice. The night he realised that the chances of their ever reconciling were finally gone, Mains lay on his bed and refused to allow himself to cry. Instead, he massaged his leg and ground his teeth and was thankful and sad and angry all at once. As he kneaded his weakened muscles, he wished his wife was with him and knew that she wouldn't ever be again and that it was the only fair way for things to be. In their conversations since then, they had never talked about Johnny.

Mornings were the worst. When Johnny had been alive, they had made an effort to always eat breakfast together as a family, sitting around the big, scratched table that had belonged originally to Mains' parents. Johnny liked cereal, the more sugar-filled the better, and Mains and Elise had constant good-natured battles with him to get him to eat something less sweet. At the weekends, they would sometimes have toast or muffins, the jam and butter on the table between them, Mains' coffee and Elise's Earl Grey tea adding scented steam to the air. After everything had happened, after Mains had left Elise and his old life behind as best he could, he had tried to be normal for a while, had tried to not be the father of a dead child or a failed husband who had left his wife. One day, he had forced himself to go to a café in the village but the smell of tea and coffee mingled around him, the odour of toasting bread and jam joined it and caught in his nose. A feeling of hopelessness came upon him in a dense and ragged wave so powerful that he had to get up and leave, swallowing back bile and something that tasted like old blood. He hadn't been back.

There were more the next day, an older couple, stooped and small and with their arms around each other, and a group of children playing. Around the group of children were new adults, looking on contentedly. It was impossible to say how he knew they were content, but they were. It was in the set of their shoulders, in the stone-chip smiles on their faces, in the relaxed slant of their eyes. And still his snowman stood apart, its face downcast as it watched the growing group below him.

It wasn't until he was walking back that Mains thought about the odd thing. Well, odd things, really. The first was that the snowpeople hadn't melted or distorted at all over the last days. The ones under the trees might escape the attentions of wind and whatever sun appeared in the day's middle hours, but his snowman did not, and should have started to shift and change. It had snowed every night and most days since he had first found the snowman and yet it remained almost the same, its features clearly defined and its shape still even and sharp. Only its arms had changed, thickening and becoming more solid so that the snowman appeared even from a distance to be reaching out, supplicant.

The other thing was that there were still no signs of human creation on any of the figures. All were smooth and regular, the ground around them unmarked. The next day, after he had looked on *more* new figures (another kissing couple, a female with a dog and child, and male and a child that appeared to be rolling the snow ahead of them to make a snowman of their own), Mains tried to build a small snowman, a snowchild to join the others, but he found that what he made was messy and ugly. The ball he rolled for its base was uneven, marred by dirt and leaves picked up from the frozen ground, its surface covered in ridges and bulges. The ground around it looked as though it had been ploughed, with great furrows tracking through the snow to the contorted thing he had created. He didn't attempt to make a face, because he suspected he already knew how it would turn out. Johnny would have loved the snowmen up here, would have loved the scenes that their unknown creator had made, and Mains didn't want to add something repugnant to them. Didn't want to add something that Johnny wouldn't have liked.

So how had the snowmen been made? Even allowing for the increased skill that came from practice, they seemed overly perfect, as though they had been formed out of the air rather than by any human intervention. It was silly, he knew, but he couldn't work out how it had been done. Perhaps they had been brought into the trees from somewhere else?

No. That would be hard, maybe impossible, to accomplish and anyway, why bother? To what end? This wasn't a popular place, wasn't on any walker's or rambler's itinerary even in the best of weathers, and in the middle of this inhospitable winter it was bleak and unforgiving. Of course, the simple explanation was that someone was coming and making the figures during the night, or later in the day after Mains had left, and the snowfall was covering their tracks and the marks of the snowpeople's making, leaving behind only these startling, wonderful figures. Walking home that day, Mains found himself grinning at the memory of them. Smiling, jolly, loving, they filled the space between the trees with a warmth that belied their cold flesh.

All except his snowman, lost and alone and out beyond their reach.

The next day, Mains woke after the first night's unbroken sleep he could remember in months. He was relaxed when he awoke, and his bed felt like a cocoon in which he had in some way grown and changed. Something about him was different, although it took him a few minutes to realise what it was—the ache in his leg was absent for the first time since the accident. He flexed it, feeling his knee click, lock, release, but thankfully not hurt. He even remembered his dreams, warm little vignettes in which he did things like made a meal, watched television and drank a beer, read a book while lying in bed. Simple things, domestic things.

As if in contrast to his relaxed mood, the weather was foul. A storm raged around the cottage, battering snow against the window in clumsy, aggressive swirls. The sky above the house, what glimpses of it Mains could find between the plunging flakes, was filled with clouds the colour and shape of roiling linen sails. The distant trees were almost lost to view, merely dark and twisting shapes whipping around under the assault, and yet after his morning coffee, Mains dressed in his warmest clothes and went out into it.

The cold was, literally, breathtaking, tearing most of the air from his mouth and nose and making his stubble brittle. It was madness, he knew, to be out in this weather, but he had to see them, to visit them again and see what new additions were there. For the first time since moving here, since the accident that mangled his leg and killed his beloved child and uncoupled him from his wife, Mains had something that he was looking forward to. He wanted to see the figures again, see them so the memory of Johnny could enjoy them, so that he could picture his son laughing at them, playing in amongst them. Even in the dank and clammy light, he knew instinctively where to go, following the paths of his previous visits surefooted and confident. Under the canopy of trees the snowstorm was less immediate, fractured into dancing swirls that escaped down between the branches to curve around the trunks and batter against his face. The falling, turning snow made new swathes across the floor, piling up into shapes like abandoned sheets. Mains went on, keeping his head hunched low into his collar and his hands thrust deep into his pockets and he walked lightly and happily.

There were no new figures. Mains was disappointed, more

disappointed than he'd expected himself to be. So whoever was making the figures had decided that the game was over; never mind. At least the other figures still remained, still hugged and kissed and played and watched. They were as clear and sharp as they had been the day before, distinct and unique and wonderful. How many of them were there in total? He didn't know. They seemed to move around him, chasing each other through the trees, playing tag and gambolling through the snow, keeping each other protected and warm. Safe.

His snowman was almost impossible to see through the storm, a darker smudge of air on the hillside beyond the trees and Mains went out to him. By the time he reached him, Mains was covered in fresh snow, corpulent flakes clinging to his jacket and legs like a new layer of skin. Close to, he saw the mouth of the snowman turned down in its now-familiar grimace and he realised that it was the same height as him. Its expression reminded him of one he saw sometimes in the mirror on his own face; not misery exactly, just a kind of hopeless bafflement. He didn't understand what had happened to his world over the previous months, and probably never would, but he could not keep from poking at its new shape, like probing the edges of a rotten tooth with a tongue that was metallic and bitter. The snowman would melt eventually, like everything; even now, it was finally losing the battle against the fresh snow, its features blurring beneath new flakes. Mains turned, intending to leave; suddenly, his fragile good mood was gone. He took several steps down the slope, and then what he saw in between the trees brought him up short.

The snowstorm was creating new shapes. The flakes were describing tight, frenzied eddies in the air between two of the nearest trunks, battering into each other and accreting into something solid, first one mass and then a second. Had there been something there for the snow to cling to? No, Mains knew that. Whatever was happening, it was happening out of the storm and from nothing else. He remembered thinking that maybe the snowpeople were forming out of the air and dismissing it as stupidity, and realised that, as stupid as it seemed, that was exactly what was happening. The shapes were becoming clearer, one larger than the other, fatter at the base than at the top, two figures made from piled spheres emerging from the dizzying melee. Figures. New snowpeople.

A woman and a child.

The female had one arm around the child and the other stretched out towards Mains. Even from this distance he could make out their faces as they formed from the blizzard, the eyes and mouth warm and wanting, the child's split into in a wide grin. The child held both its arms out towards Mains, and as he watched more features form—ears and noses, the suggestion of hair on the female's head, a hat like Johnny used to wear on the child's, scarves around both necks—still they reached out to Mains.

To Mains? No, he realised, not to him; to the snowman behind him. He turned back to it, only to find that its face was lost now, that its eyes and mouth were covered in new snow and it couldn't see the couple beckoning to him. Mains panicked, startled himself by screaming and running back up the slope, reaching up and wiping frenziedly at the fresh flakes, clearing them so that the snowman's eyes were revealed and it could see his lover and child. Its face still hadn't changed, was still so sad, had been made only for sorrow, and before he knew what he was doing Mains was taking the stones that formed its mouth and thrusting them into his own mouth. His teeth splintered and shattered and he felt the bright flare of pain but it was the smallest thing really, a candle-flame of discomfort trying to stand against the swelling wave of joy he felt. He did not have to force the smile that came, wide and bloody, to his lips. The last thing he saw before he replaced his eyes with the chips of dark stone was the snow covering him completely, recreating him, and then he was running down the slope and into an embrace, two embraces, as warm as any he had ever known and it felt like coming home.

MAMI WATA

THE HEAT WAS like a brick.

Thorley had never seen shadows like it; they seemed edged in gold and darker at their centre than pitch. Even indoors, they pooled at his feet like glorious ink, gathering around his ankles and under the tables in the chibuku tavern. They even reflected themselves in the sweat that gathered on the brow of Chilongo, Thorley's companion seated on the other side of the table.

"This is a good place," Chilongo was saying. "An honest place. Sure, we have our problems, like anywhere, but we've always worked hard. I don't know why they had to send you."

"They sent me," said Thorley, "because the mine's production has fallen by over half and they want to know why." Behind Chilongo, bottles glittered on the shelves lining the bar, throwing their own shadows across the mural painted onto the wall—a mermaid, golden haired and naked, back to the bar's interior but looking over her shoulder into the room. Her tail was splayed out in front of her, half-hidden by her body. Beyond, painted smaller so that they looked insignificant and weak, were rows of men. They looked awestruck, frightened.

Actually, Thorley hadn't been sent, he had chosen to come, even though he didn't need to. The loss of production was a financial concern but it could have been sorted out by phone and email with the onsite managers. It was Chilongo's voice that had done it in the end, its rich musicality dancing down the telephone line and making the already grey British day greyer. Thorley had heard the sun in Chilongo's voice, heard the rhythms of African speech, heard something brighter than the drear that faced him through the window, and it had called to him, irresistible and powerful.

"Every mine has runs of luck, good and bad," said Chilongo. "We've just hit a bad period."

"Indeed?" said Thorley. "And yet the last report said shaft four had hit a new seam, and was promising great dividends."

"It didn't play out," insisted Chilongo. "It looked good, but then it turned out to be nothing. We've had some flooding in the deepest shaft, some machinery problems. Nothing to worry about. You know how it goes."

"No," said Thorley, "I don't." And as he said it he thought to himself, *But I know when someone's lying to me. What I don't know is why.*

Thorley had decided not to stay in one of the large hotels. Travelling in from Kitwe, the town nearest to the mine, would have been a waste and besides, he wanted to see what industrial Zambia was really like. He had seen the brochures that sometimes came across his desk, glossy things filled with pictures of wild animals and wide, sweeping plains, telling prospective investors about the landscape and the abundant workforce and the stable government, and about mines that produced yield after impressive yearly yield of copper or nickel or cobalt, but he had never visited. He had never needed to; previously, things had run smoothly and the local managers had dealt with everything. He also didn't want to stay with the expats, although several of them had offered him accommodation when they discovered he was coming. He had never liked expat communities, which seemed to him to fall too easily into patterns of casual racism redolent of colonialism. They were a necessary evil as Thorley saw it, useful for the skills pool they provided but claustrophobic with nostalgia and boredom, and he certainly didn't need to expose himself to it any more than was strictly necessary. Instead, he had chosen to stay in a workers' motel on the outskirts of Kitwe, not far from the mine.

Thorley could have been in a room anywhere—there was a bed with nondescript covers and sagging mattress, cheap sideboard that doubled as a television stand, shower room created by partitioning off one corner and installing a plastic cubicle and shower, and a chair on which he hung his clothes. He placed his underwear and shirts in the sideboard drawers, seeing as he did so a Gideon's *Bible*. It was old, bleached by the heat, and its spine cracked painfully when he lifted and opened it, the imitation leather dry and brittle. The drawers were lined with newspaper, he saw, aged to the colour of sand and as brittle as the Gideon's spine. He lifted out a sheet and tried to read it, but the print had faded so that he could only make out some of the words. The headline on the page read FOUR DEAD MEN and below was a date in July, three months previous. He put the sheet back in the drawer and decided to work.

Even after sundown, the heat was oppressive. The motel had no air conditioning, and Thorley soon found that the only way to stay even close to comfortable was to strip to his pants and fan himself with the papers he was supposed to be reading. It was impossible to concentrate anyway; he knew most of the facts already, about how the mine's production had fallen off dramatically in the previous five months, down from around four hundred fifty tonnes to less than three hundred, and how there was no official explanation (apart from Chilongo's "bad luck") for this drop in output. Much of the explanation, Thorley saw, would lie in the significant drop in workforce numbers that had occurred over the previous months. The mine still operated, of course; they had not lost that many men, just more than was normal or usual, for reasons that weren't clear.

Thorley could hear the mine workings as he lay on his bed, a distant throatless rumble peaking occasionally into dull booms or percussive echoes. Closer to, someone was playing a radio loud, the signal fading in and out so that the music and voices seemed to sway about Thorley. He was exhausted and hot, his eyes gritty from tiredness and the dry air, his sweat lying across him like a second skin. The tapwater was only lukewarm and did not quench his thirst, no matter how much he drank. He was wondering about dressing and going in search of ice when he must have, finally, drifted into slumber.

When Thorley awoke it was still dark, and not much cooler. He sat up, realising as he did so that some of his papers had stuck to his body. They peeled off with a sound like kissing, leaving the ghosts of letters on his flesh that rubbed away under his fingers. In the distance, he heard sirens, or one siren echoing, it was hard to tell, and men shouting. He went to the window of his room, picking up his glass of tepid water on the way, and pulled aside the curtains. His rented car was a grey shape in the darkness, and the flat apron of the car park beyond a smooth shadow segmented by painted lines. Despite the noises, which seemed to be getting closer, he could see no movement except the distant shimmer of thorn bushes moving in the slight breeze.

Actually, that wasn't quite true. The far edge of the car park bordered the road to the mine, and now he could see someone walking along it, heading away from the motel. Shadows from the buildings on the far side of the road swept across the figure as it walked, an alternating, dappling pattern. It was a woman, Thorley saw, tall and thin and white with straggly blonde hair that fell down her naked back.

Naked? No, that couldn't be right. She must surely have some backless top or dress on, something cool for this stifling heat. He couldn't see her lower half, so shrouded in shadow was she, but he thought he could hear the swish of material as she walked. Just before she walked out of view, an ambulance went past heading away from the mine, its swirling light illuminating her fully for a moment, showing Thorley her long arms and splayed hands with dark nails. In the moment of her disappearance, she turned her face to him and smiled, her teeth white as alabaster against the surrounding night. She was young, and very pretty.

The next morning, Thorley ate breakfast and waited for Chilongo. The motel had no dining room, so he had walked over the road to a tavern that had a sign outside advertising *Good Food From Early Till Late* and ordered himself a coffee and the fruit plate. Although it was before eight, the sun had already cast itself hard across the ground, creating more of those shadows that seemed so dark. It was worse inside the tavern, where the large glass windows, clouded with dust and dirt though they were, magnified the heat of the morning far beyond anything the slowly turning ceiling fan could cope with. Flies buzzed across the trays of wild mango, plum, and sand apple, the owner flicking a red cloth at them half-heartedly, making them rise and fall.

Thorley sat at the table farthest from the windows, hoping to find some respite from the light. At a nearby table, two men stared with undisguised interest at him. He smiled, nodded, broke eye contact by looking down at the papers he had brought with him. The coffee was poor, weak and gruel-like, but the fruit was excellent, fleshy and juicy and, to his palate, exotic, and he enjoyed the sensation and taste of it. As he ate, he looked around the tavern. The other diners were mostly men, workers from the mine he assumed, some coming off nightshift, others going on. The men going on shift, cleaner and fresher, ate fruit and spoke to each other; the men coming off shift ate plates of vegetables and meat in silence. Most of the men looked over at him during their meals, eyes sullen and wary.

Behind the counter and counterman, painted on the rear wall, was a mural. This one showed a dark-skinned woman with long hair confidently facing into the room, with a comb in one hand. She was naked apart from a snake, draped around her shoulders, its tail and head covering her breasts. The artist had painted her well, and she glowed with large, expressive eyes and a ripe, full mouth. The landscape behind her, however, was cruder, showing only the barest of detail. Hills and a vast plain stretched out, the plain full of what Thorley first thought were apes or horses but then realised were men. There were hundreds of them, mostly barely more than stick figures, all facing the woman. Some appeared to be kneeling, others had their arms raised. It was an odd mix of primitive and modern art styles, although an impressive one.

Chilongo appeared late, stressed but apologetic, and with some of the dancing cadences gone from his voice. He was tired, Thorley saw, the bruised flesh under his eyes sagging and dark. The man was rumpled, his clothes creased. Rings of sweat, dried and fresh, gathered under his shirtsleeves. He smelled anxious and sour.

"I am so sorry," he said. "It has been a difficult morning and I was unavoidably delayed."

"Problem?" Thorley asked.

"No. Well, yes," said Chilongo. "There was an incident last night, and one of the men died. One of the miners, I mean. He was in another motel, like yours, and he was found dead."

"Not an incident at the mine? An accident, I mean, onsite?"

"No."

"Then why should that be a problem for you?" asked Thorley.

"Because," said Chilongo, "I am the man in charge of the miners and of the visitors to the mine. I am responsible for them." He sounded angry, indignant, and Thorley raised a placatory hand, motioning Chilongo to sit.

"Sorry," he said, "I meant no offence. Now, we have a long few days ahead of us. Please, take me to the mine and you can tell me what's been happening on the way."

"We like to keep visitors away," said Chilongo, noticing Thorley wince as they bounced across yet another rut over the deteriorated track that led to the small mine, a smaller site, specialising in the deepest seams. "Originally, it was to keep ourselves insignificant in the eyes of others, so that they would not bother us. The larger companies are not above having their trucks deliberately break down to block access, or staging the accidental shedding of loads of trash in awkward places, if they perceive you as a threat. Now, however, it stops the inquisitive attempting to get onsite. Reporters and the like."

"Reporters? Why reporters?"

"Because of the deaths."

The mine, even though small by comparison with some of the others scattered across the copperbelt, was still huge. As they juddered along the road, and through two security checkpoints, Thorley waited to see the investment he was here to protect. He wasn't sure what he expected, exactly; a series of sheds around a caged lifthead, possibly, or a carved expanse of parched earth hollowed out from the ground, but in reality it was neither. It was a complicated, layered series of huts and prefab buildings, of varying heights, built in the centre of a vast, dusty plain. The separate structures were clustered together, creating the impression of a huge, ever-expanding castle, sprawling its way across the earth like some creeping, cancerous thing. As they drew close, Thorley saw the individual huts were huge, boxy structures painted green and brown and coated in sand and dirt, their fronts open to allow trucks to drive in and out.

More trucks and dirty buildings lined the perimeter. The buildings were strangely shaped, with sloped roofs or walls that were missing entirely, all of them linked by rumbling, moving multi-layered conveyor belts like arteries. All over the site, chimneys pierced the air, stretching up from the ground and loosing spiralling coils of dirty grey smoke into the sky. Thorley enjoyed the size of it, could feel the vibration of the machinery even in the car. Even with the windows closed, he smelled the sharp stench of acid and machinery and burning, could hear the lupine growl of the conveyor belts and smelting units. He turned to Chilongo, wanting to say something about the sheer immensity of what he was seeing and hearing, but saw that the other man was looking at the approaching mineworks with a strange expression on his face—he looked scared.

Thorley spent the day going through the mine's records, interviewing the managers and supervisors. He soon realised that there was a distinct split in attitude between those staff who worked solely overground, mainly the expat managers, and those who went underground, mostly locals or supervisors brought in from other areas. The managers put the fall in production down to worker greed, blaming miners who had slowed down or left in the hope of getting higher pay, shorter hours or more benefits. They showed him lengthy technical reports, most written by the same expat managers that were showing them to him, full of technical dialogue and graphs and phrases like *unexpected seam depletion* and *shaft misalignment*, none of which told him anything. In one he came across the phrase *envirocultural factors having an impact upon workforce cohesion and permanence*, but it was not clear what this meant. The workers who went underground all reported variations on a theme—the mine was simply "unlucky".

That night, Chilongo took Thorley to a different tavern to eat, this one closer to Kitwe. It looked to have been built out of an old barn, but the inside was nicely decorated and the tables were large and spaced far enough apart that Thorley didn't feel overlooked or overheard. The meal was pleasant, and although he had little inclination to talk to Chilongo, the other man seemed to have recovered some of his energy since the morning and spoke enough for both of them. Thorley listened only partially, chewing his food and glancing around. This was a place couples came, and although it was only early evening, there were several pairs dining around the room. Most looked at him, some fleetingly, some with longer, more intense stares. The couple nearest to him held a fierce, whispered conversation, clearly about him; Thorley caught the word *muzungu* once or twice. He had heard it this morning at breakfast as well, and the previous day, never spoken to his face.

"It means 'westerner'," said Chilongo. "That word you keep hearing. We are used to foreigners here, of course, but you are clearly not a mine operator and you have arrived at a bad time. It makes people nervous."

"How can you tell I'm not a mine operator?" asked Thorley, intrigued.

"Ha! You are soft-looking, as though you have spent your life behind a desk. Mine operators, underground or over-ground, tend to look like the thing they mine eventually. Hard, in the case of copper. Even when a miner is clean, he looks crusted with dirt, no?"

Thorley nodded; it was true. He had met miners ten years into their retirement and they still appeared as though their skin was grainy with cinders and grit.

"You aren't dirty. To miners and the people that know them, you don't look as if you've ever been dirty in your life."

"Why is this a difficult time? Because of the deaths?"

Chilongo didn't answer straight away, but took a sip of his pulpy elephant orange drink—what he called *Muhulu-hulu*, crunching on an icecube. "The deaths are part of it," he said eventually. "A small part. It's not easy to explain. This isn't a happy place now, or at least, not as happy as it was. But working towns are never that happy, are they? Always worried about production or closures or being undersold, or accidents, or death. There's no one here who isn't related to a miner, or a trucker or a boss or a guard for the mine. The expats tell us to get on with the work, but they don't understand either."

"Understand what?"

"Are you still planning to come underground tomorrow, to see the mine in operation?" Thorley nodded.

"Then maybe you'll see then."

His motel room was no cooler that evening, although Thorley had managed to get a bucket of ice from reception and had dropped two bottles of water into it in the hope that they would stay chilled for the night. He had also bought himself Scotch whiskey and drunk several shots after returning from his meal. But all he could think about was that Chilongo was hiding something, that was for sure, and the mine managers had no idea of what was happening. Despite all the reports and conversations today, he was no clearer about why this mine was losing staff, and had falling production figures. They paid well and were generous employers, the conditions were no worse than any of the other companies working in the area and better than some, and yet people were walking away from their jobs. Six percent of the workforce last month, four percent the month before, seven the month before that, and few were being replaced. The positions were being advertised, but there were few if any applicants. It made no sense. None.

The car park was fuller tonight, Thorley saw. As well as his own rental Toyota, already picking up a thin layer of sand and dust after only a day's disuse, there were two jeeps with mine company logos and four other cars. The radio was playing again, its indistinct tones tonight accompanied by singing, although whether by a man or woman Thorley could not tell. People were drinking in other rooms, he knew; there had already been one shouted argument, the voices slurred, and a bout of raucous laughter that ended in the sound of a bottle breaking. Thorley sipped his whiskey and waited for the world to cool.

At just before midnight, the woman appeared again. She walked into Thorley's view on the far side of the car park, this time coming from the mine rather than walking towards it. In the sodium orange of the streetlights, her skin seemed the colour of mocha and her auburn hair gleamed like the copper he had spent the day investigating. She walked across the road to the edge of the concrete apron and then stopped, appearing to stare at him even though she was surely too far away to see him. There was something enticing in her gaze, even at this distance, something feral and erotic. Thorley became uncomfortably aware that he was standing at the window wearing only boxers and with a growing erection. Stepping back into the shadows of the room, he continued watching. The woman began to walk across the car park, and although he couldn't see her lower half because of the cars and jeep between her and him, he suddenly became convinced she was naked. He could see the sweep of her clavicles and neck, her hair framing a rounded, attractive face and dropping away down a chest he was suddenly sure was bare. He could see no t-shirt neckline or blouse collars, no thin vest straps or bandeau top.

When the man came into view and saw the woman, he was as surprised as Thorley was. Drunk, he swayed as he walked, was scrabbling in his pockets for something, head down and oblivious. The woman turned towards the new man, his skin dark and sweating in the humid night, and smiled broadly. He, seeing her, took two stumbling steps back and then turned and staggered back the way he had come. With a last look towards Thorley, she shifted direction, following the other man. Thorley watched her go, somewhere between disappointed and glad; his visit here was complicated enough without adding a woman into the scenario. Finishing his whiskey, he went to bed. It was only later, as he drifted towards sleep, that Thorley realised that the woman had been blonde the night before.

She could easily have dyed her hair, he thought the next morning. People did, after all. It wasn't unusual. Looking around the tavern, he saw that, of the two of the women in there, one had plaits woven into her hair, making it a tangle of straw blonde, red and black that framed her dark face like a halo. Thorley lifted another piece of papaya into his mouth, gazing again at the mural.

"She is beautiful, yes?" said a voice. Thorley looked around to find Chilongo standing at his side. "*Mami Wata.* Water mother. You will find her in most of the bars and taverns in the copperbelt. Across large parts of Africa, really."

"Are they all pictures of her? All the different women in the murals?"

"They are all versions of her. She lives in our bars because she attracts men, and where men come, they want to drink. She likes the noise and the attention."

Thorley raised his eyes to Chilongo; he was staring at the woman on the wall with a look on his face that Thorley could not completely recognise, a mix of fascination and anger and something else. Lust, maybe. Looking again at the mural, he realised that the mermaid reminded him of the woman from the midnight street.

Outside, the dusty pavement glowed a heated yellow in the glare of the early morning sun. The road, a strip of darker tarmac, glinted as Thorley and Chilongo walked across it. It was already hot enough to create ripples in the air that Thorley could *feel*, warm pulsations that tickled his ankles.

Crossing towards Chilongo's car, Thorley saw a crowd gathering in a loose, mutating cluster a couple of hundred yards away.

"What's happening?" asked Thorley.

"Nothing," said Chilongo. He kept his eyes fixed on the car, and it seemed to Thorley that his companion was deliberately not looking at the crowd.

"Nothing?" he asked.

"Nothing. Come, we have to get you underground."

The lift cage was empty, but it smelled of men, muscular, sweaty, exhausted. Chilongo and one of the mine engineers, a dark-bearded expat named Rowe, checked each others' equipment one last time and then closed the doors for descent.

"We're going to almost the deepest point in the mine, to one of the newer shafts, so that you can observe the operation and maybe talk to some of the men," said Rowe as though this was news to Thorley, as though he hadn't been the one who requested this excursion. *Take me deep*, he had said, *and let me talk to the miners. I need to know what the problem is.* It was clear Rowe didn't like him, or didn't trust him. Thorley could see it in the looks that were even now surreptitiously coming his way. He had the impression that Rowe and Chilongo didn't like each other, but now Rowe was talking to Chilongo as though they were friends, pointedly excluding Thorley. Thorley didn't really mind; it gave him a chance to look around. It was several years since he had been underground, but he found he still enjoyed it. The temperature drop as they descended was satisfying, as if they were escaping the raw heat of the day above, diving into some cooling swathe that refreshed rather than chilled. He

128

liked the sound of the lift, the metallic clatter dancing above the rumble of the motor and the fainter sound of the mine's working belly. He even liked the feel of the clothes he had changed into and the weight of the helmet on his head.

When the descent was over, the lift opened out into a wide shaft that went in both directions, sloping down and echoing with voices and the clank of machinery. Lights were strung out in cabled lines along the tunnel, the air around them haloed in dust and hanging moisture. Two conveyor belts, one above the other, ran along the centre of the tunnel. Both were currently motionless, the heavy rubber belts empty apart from streaks of crushed earth and dry, friable rock fragments. Down here, the change in air pressure made Thorley's ears ache slightly. The smell had changed, from the strong male odour of the lift to one of burning rock and the heavy, tarry scent of oil and exhaust fumes. The three walked down the tunnel, passing under ribs of heavy wood and tight cabling. The noise grew louder as they walked until talking to each became almost impossible. At one point, Chilongo stopped Thorley and pointed down an unlit side tunnel

"It is the flooded one, the deep one," he shouted. "It did not play out, and we had water problems. It is why our production fell so far."

No, thought Thorley, *it's not.* One failed excursion should not have affected output that dramatically, despite what Chilongo said. The mine was always sending out exploratory shoots, some of which played out and some of which did not. It was normal behaviour. But something else was going on here.

They came upon the man about ten minutes after passing the abandoned deep shaft. He was positioned under one of the lights, peering intently back up along the tunnel. Under his covering of dirt and sweat, it was near-impossible to tell if he was black or white. Only his eyes, gleaming white against the grime on his face, showed clearly. When he saw them, the man started, stepping back away from the light and into one of the shadowed areas between the bulbs.

"You! Come here! What are you doing?" Rowe demanded.

"Watching," said the man.

"Watching? For what?" Rowe shouted and Thorley could feel the anger coming from him, fury that showed itself in his bared teeth and reddening face.

"Watching," repeated the man. Chilongo nodded at him and drew Rowe aside, leaning into his ear and speaking too fast and low for Thorley to hear. Feeling his own anger build, he stepped after them, trying to discern what the Zambian was saying. Chilongo, seeing him, broke off and shouted, with forced cheerfulness, "Let us go. We are almost there."

The large gang of men were working on a new shaft, operating a huge excavator. Water sprayed against the rock face, massive blades chewing into it and spitting the savaged chunks out behind where they were taken by smaller belts to be sorted and disposed of. The noise was nearly unbearable, even through Thorley's ear protectors, a constant roar of tortured stone and the grind of machinery and the gearshift crunch of an engine labouring under huge pressure merging with the reptile hiss of the water and men calling to each other. The sound was a physical thing, the air vibrating and beating against Thorley's clothes and exposed skin in a tattoo of industrial rhythms.

Dust was hanging in the air, reducing the light to a murky yellow gleam punctuated by bright spotlights on the excavator and the paler eyes of the helmet lamps. Rowe, leaving Chilongo and Thorley, went to find the supervisor, going from man to anonymous man to locate him. He was on his way back towards them, pulling a smaller man with him, when the man from the main tunnel reappeared. He was running, banging into Thorley as he dashed past, leaping up onto the running board of the excavator and screaming at the operator. In a moment, the machine fell silent and still, the men shouting and rushing around. Lights clicked off, the sudden darkness shocking in its intensity. Thorley heard Rowe shout something and then Chilongo was at Thorley's side and reaching up to turn his helmet lamp off. Thorley wanted to speak, to reach up and switch the lamp back on, but Chilongo gripped his hand tightly and said, "Leave it. Stay silent. Please." Rowe shouted again and as the last of the lights went off, Thorley saw one of the miners wrap a hand around his mouth and drag him to the floor. "You will be safe if you stay silent and still," said Chilongo. "Please, trust me."

The darkness, now complete, brought with it silence. Thorley tried to move but Chilongo pulled him back against the rough wall, tightening his grip on Thorley's hand as he did so. Thorley, recognising that he was powerless, submitted and remained still.

The first sound was a frictional rustle. It was very faint at first but grew rapidly louder, a constantly shifting, moving sound that made Thorley think of heavy drapes in a breeze or a taffeta ballgown wrapped around a dancing woman's thighs. Under it there was something else, a clink like stones being tapped together or teeth clicking. Surrounded by the blackness of the absolute, Thorley could not help but populate the darkness with shapes, although he did not know what the shapes were. Something was even now slipping around the corner, heading towards them, he was sure. The noise was growing louder, sounding less like material, becoming more like paws stepping delicately over uneven ground or scales rasping against stone. A new scent came to Thorley's nostrils, fetid and sour like water that cannot flow.

Something moved in the darkness before Thorley's face. He felt the air shift as it went past, and his face prickled with fevered heat.

Towards the excavator, one of the men whimpered and the thing in the darkness darted away, snapping like a whipping canvas sail in the feverish air. Something skittered away from him, the chitinous clatter not quite covering a noise like some subtle beast scenting the air.

Another man whispered something before being shushed, and the air shifted once more as the thing moved, swift and invisible, among the group. A third man let out a stifled cry and then a fourth, (*Rowe*, Thorley thought), moaned. Another movement, another displacement of air and a hollow, terrible sucking. Rowe groaned again and one of the other men shouted. Someone screamed, the panic echoing as the sucking came again, and Rowe let out a rattled breath. Thorley realised that Chilongo was pulling at him, that he had stepped forward without knowing why, and then the air moved again and the burning heat caressed his cheek once more. Chilongo yanked him once and he was falling, banging, careening into the darkness as something wheeled back towards the main tunnel.

"What was it?"

Chilongo did not answer, but merely shook his head.

"An animal? *A lion in the tunnels?*" asked Thorley, insistent. The sun caught in the sweat on Chilongo's face, birthing shadows around his eyes.

They were in the workers' canteen, above ground and alone. The rest of the shift had gone, and Rowe had been taken home. Their exit from the tunnel had been frantic and confused, all shouts and pushes and pulls, carrying the half-conscious Rowe and looking around as they ran, stumbling across uneven floors and past side tunnels that yawned like expectant mouths. They had not turned on the main lights before fleeing, using only the lamps of their helmets, the hazy beams crossing and crisscrossing in the wide tunnel, illuminating men running gracelessly on all sides of him, heading back up the slope. Even in the lift, claustrophobic and full, Thorley couldn't relax, but stared through the lattice of the closed door as it began to rise, half-expecting to see something appearing from the darkness to snatch them back into the gloom.

Nothing came.

Rowe was not injured that Thorley could see, although he seemed exhausted and dopey, as though he had heatstroke. One of the other managers had agreed to drive him home and Thorley had watched as the supervisor was taken to the car, walking like an old man. He seemed thinner, somehow, as though being underground had wasted him in some way. Even his shadow looked old, grey and brittle and shrunken, and not the depthless and expansive black of the shadows of the man who escorted him or the surrounding cars and buildings.

"It is not an animal," the African said finally. "It is something else. A tourist, really. She has come like a snake from one of the lakes, Kashiba or Namulolobwe perhaps, and is merely enjoying a change of scenery. It has happened before. She never stays long. It is nearly over and she will move on soon, find somewhere new to be. It's said Mobutu kept her, or one like her, in the Congo, and she gave him strength and jewels for thirty years."

"She? It's a woman?" asked Thorley.

"Not a woman, no," said Chilongo. From over his shoulder, another painted mermaid stared at Thorley. *Even here,* he thought, although this picture was like cave art. In it, the mermaid, with a fat serpent wound around her body, was grinning widely and holding up a hand upon which a stick figure danced. The figure was male, had swollen genitalia but no facial features. The mermaid's breasts were exposed, full and rounded, with dark, prominent nipples. She was pale, almost white, with red hair.

"If not a woman, then what?" asked Thorley.

"*Mami Wata,*" said Chilongo. "A water demon."

Thorley finished his whiskey whilst making the call. Yes, the mine had suffered some local staffing problems, he said, but they were on their way to being sorted. Production would rise again soon. Chilongo and Rowe had been the very essence of helpfulness, showing him what he needed to see. All was well in Zambia...

He didn't believe it.

He wasn't sure what was happening here, but he knew he would never get to the bottom of it. He saw it in the suspicion on the faces of the mineworkers, heard it in the voices of the others eating in the taverns, felt it in the heat and in Chilongo's deferential touch to his shoulder as he got out of the car. "Go back," Chilongo had said. "Go back and leave us to finish this. It is nearly over, she has almost all she wants. Things will be well again soon." Thorley could see no other course of action; demon or animal, imagination or reality, he had no way to understand what was happening here and no strategy for dealing with it. His own places were calling him now, where the shadows weren't so dark, and the streets were slick and definable and dull. He wanted to go home.

—.—

It was late on Thorley's last night in Zambia. A frantic scratching was beckoning him from a heated sleep, as he lay on top of cheap blankets that stuck to his skin. Clad only in his shorts, he went to the window and drew back the curtains.

The woman was on the other side of the glass.

She smiled. Thorley's original suspicions were right; she was naked, her breasts pressed flat against the pane. One hand was also flattened against the glass, the fingers scratching at it slowly. In the darkness, her skin seemed to shift from a rich, lustred brown to a pale pink, and her hair shimmered from black to blonde. Her smile showed teeth as white as milk, her eyes dark and feral and inviting. Thorley stepped away from the window, uncomfortably aware of his stiffening erection. Her incisors were long, gleaming against pomegranate-red lips, the nails on the end of her fingers curved into wicked hooks. Her areolae were perfect circles and he knew that if he stepped close enough and looked down, he would see that her legs were long and shapely, meeting in a delta of musky hair. He stepped towards the door, pulling off his shorts as he went.

Outside, a slight breeze blew air that was warmer and dry against Thorley's naked flesh. The woman came to him, holding her arms out, naked as he'd expected and hoped, her tongue poking out slightly from between enticing lips. Thorley stepped into the cage of her arms, feeling himself tremble. She made a noise like a hissing snake and her smile widened so that it seemed to crawl around her entire face and her mouth opened and that tongue came out, long and red and black and curling and tasting the air, tasting *him*, and then Chilongo rasped, "Leave him be."

He was standing just out of the woman's reach, holding a shotgun and pointing it at her. "He is *muzungu*. Taking him will mean trouble. Find another."

The woman hissed again and Thorley suddenly wondered how he had seen her as attractive. She smelled wild, of earth and urine and spoiled meat and her tongue was longer than any had a right to be, her only sound a hiss, instinctive and vicious. He stepped back but she moved with him, stepping to follow him, staring at him. Chilongo moved forwards, pushing the gun barrel into her belly and saying, "No. *Fingi!* Go into the town, there are men there who will only be missed by us, not by anyone else."

Her tongue was on his skin, wet and warm, slipping against his neck. Chilongo pushed with the barrel and she moved, opening her arms and releasing Thorley. She glared at Chilongo, who gestured briefly with the shotgun towards the road. Away from her, the smell of her dissipating, Thorley was aroused again as he looked at her breasts, at the way her lips were parted and her breath came in tiny gasps. Chilongo looked across at him and said, "Go. She is not for you, nor you her." As if in reply, the woman sibilated, low and venomous, and her tongue appeared again, lapping at the air. Revulsion washed across him and he backed away.

Thorley managed to stumble to his room as the woman, the *thing*, remained motionless, staring at Chilongo. He met her gaze without moving, the gun barrel's black maw hovering at the height of her belly. On the far side of the car park a car sped past, horn braying. Chilongo, distracted, glanced away and in the briefest moment that his eyes were averted, the woman moved.

She covered the distance to Chilongo incredibly fast, dropping low as she went and shrieking like wind across glass bottles. As the car moved along the road, Chilongo's shadow shifted around him, dancing with the moving headlights, and the woman went with it. Her face brushed the ground, the scraped-porcelain noise of her teeth grinding across the pavement making Thorley's own teeth ache in sympathy. Her tongue lashed at the ground ahead of her face, writhing and lapping at Chilongo's shade, sucking violently. Chilongo let out a scream, high and thin, and took two steps forwards, wobbling. The woman darted away from the African, rising as she did so, licking tendrils of blackness that dangled from her mouth and dripped across her breasts. Chilongo fell to his knees and gave a last, weak exhalation. He looked across at Thorley, and Thorley saw tears glittering in his eyes as he fell forwards, his head cracking against the floor. Thorley slammed his room door shut, backed away further until his knees hit the bed and he fell across it. Ignoring the terrible, liquid sucking sounds coming from outside, he pulled the blanket around him so that it covered his head and thought about home.

The sounds carried on for a long time, impossible to avoid, too audible, slithering into his ears like old grease. Thorley curled up, pulling his knees into a foetal position and wrapping his arms around his legs. The rough grey blanket prickled against this skin as he prayed for the noises to stop.

In the morning, Chilongo was still there. Thorley hadn't slept; dressing quickly, packing and leaving the motel room early before anyone in the rooms around him stirred. He saw the man's body was in the same place, legs on the road and head towards Thorley's door. Kneeling beside Chilongo, he looked into his glassy, dead eyes and said a silent thank you. The low rising sun glared into his face as he rose, and he saw that Chilongo was the only thing in the car park not casting a shadow. He went to his car, throwing his bag in the rear seat, and drove away quickly.

He did not look back, but he did drive to the mine. The smelting works and storage units and the spiderweb connections of conveyor belts and ramps twisted around him as he wound to the front of the main building and parked. Thorley got out of his car, sensing the difference in this place. He walked out to the centre of the open space, looking around him. The air burned hot with the acidic scour of industry. All was busier than it had been on his previous visits despite the early hour. Two men, crossing the dusty apron to the lorries parked on the far side, laughed. Machinery roared, its volume shivering the dust hanging in the air. The mine pulsed with energy and movement and life. Whatever she was, whatever darkness had been deep in the belly of the mine, had gone. Suddenly exhausted, Thorley turned and moved back towards the car. It was time to go.

As the rental limped down the road, he saw in the rear-view mirror the towering battlements and turrets of the mine, the chimneys spewing ropes of smoke into the morning air, curled like snakes against the sun.

THE SEVEN PEOPLE YOU
DON'T MEET TODAY

FIRST WEEK

MONDAY: TURN FACE Lady almost smiled at him. He could see it in her eyes and playing at the corners of her mouth as she glanced across at him, making Channing grin as she tried to deny her feelings.

It was simple; he liked to imagine that Turn Face Lady, who he always passed somewhere around the end of his road, found him attractive. Clearly she couldn't admit it, even to herself, so she deliberately avoided looking at him, never making eye contact or smiling, only ever glancing rapidly from downcast eyes. A classic case of denial if ever he saw one.

By contrast, Old Lady Walker liked him and wasn't afraid to admit it. He saw her this morning, as most mornings, near the crossing that led to the river path and, as ever, she smiled broadly at him as she strode forcefully along and swung her arms in time with her feet. He imagined she had picked walking as her daily exercise, as evidenced by her stout boots and sensible coat, and seeing him brightened her day up. Maybe he reminded her of someone from her youth; a lover, perhaps, or even a husband. Maybe a son. Whatever, she liked him and smiled and he always smiled back.

The Gimp pretended he didn't exist. Channing had decided long ago that this was because he was concentrating on staying upright and mobile and in charge of his lurching body. The Gimp's arm was twisted across his belly and he limped heavily as he walked, favouring his left side, so that Channing always overtook him somewhere on the first stretch of path along the side of the river. Once, he had nodded at The Gimp in greeting but had been ignored so he had not bothered since, and this morning was no different. The Gimp, head down and with a rolling gait, did not look up as Channing passed by.

At least The Gimp wasn't as sour-faced as Grumpy Bike Lady, who Channing saw towards the end of the path. She was small and hunched, bent over the handlebars of a cycle that appeared far too big for her. Most mornings, there was fruit in the basket on its front and a look of sheer, miserable determination on her face. She travelled in the opposite direction to Channing and most days he saw her coming, giving him the chance to get out of her way. The unhappiness and exertion on her face, made obvious by the deep lines across her forehead and around her downturned mouth, made him think that her course was set and not open to deviation or negotiation, and that if he did not move, she would knock him out of the way. She hated cycling, he was sure, and he never said hello to her or smiled at her because it would seem as though he were rubbing her nose in it: *See, I can be cheerful! I have time to look around at this glorious riverside scenery whilst you pedal your hated machine and simply see the ground ahead of you.*

This morning, Rockabilly Boy was behind Grumpy Bike Lady although he was sometimes ahead of her. His razor-sharp sideburns and perfect quiff never seemed affected by the weather or by the fact that he, too, was on a pushbike. Channing could fathom little about the man other than he was young, and he paid attention to his appearance. No one who had hair like that or who shaved so carefully could be considered slovenly. He would sometimes nod at Channing, but did not this morning.

Dog Man usually came in to view as Channing started on the final approach to the train station, his mongrel dog trotting at his heel, a ball wedged firmly in its mouth. Dog Man always said *Hello* out loud to Channing, the only person on his daily walk that did so. He was elderly but spritely, his pace fast so that he and Channing only saw each other for a few minutes each day. Channing always said hello back to Dog Man, enjoying the sense of comradeship that the little contact gave him.

And then there was the seventh. When Channing arrived at the station, he looked around hopefully for Smiling Girl and, as she had been since he first moved here and started this commute, she smiled at him. Short, slim and dark, she waited on the same platform as he did but boarded the earlier train, and she always smiled at him. Of all the seven regulars Channing saw on his morning walk, Smiling Lady was the only one he ever considered striking up a conversation with; she seemed genuinely to like him, was pleased to see him, and he definitely liked her. *One day*, he told himself, *one day, but not today*. Today, she could remain Smiling Girl who might conceivably like him. If he spoke to her and she turned out to simply smile, and not like him, he would have to change her to something like Tease Girl, and he had no desire to do that. The machine of his life was running smooth, he was in control, and he liked what he had; a new life in a new town, a good job running small projects for the regional arm of a multinational company, money and few responsibilities.

That Monday morning, Channing was told that he had finally been allocated a leadership role on an important project, one that could really get him noticed, and boost his movement up the corporate ladder. It was why he had uprooted himself from the place he had lived all his life, left his family and friends and moved here. And now, here it was. At last! It was a good day.

Tuesday: It was a joke that had turned into a superstition, really. Channing walked the two miles to the train station every day and he had found the journey exciting and refreshing when he first started, but now it was mostly boring. There were only so many times you could see the early sun reflecting off the river, see herons sleeping on the rocks and mud flats, watch ducks dive for fish, before those sights lost their lustre. This was his commute, better than some to be sure, but still dull and grinding and unwanted. And so, his seven markers had been born; the seven people he passed regularly on his journey and who he measured his journey by. Over time, he had come to the joking conclusion that they were his harbingers of good fortune; if they were all there, that was good news and he would have a good day. One or two missing (running late, or on holiday maybe) could be dealt with, three or more of them gone meant a bad day was in the offing. They were like pistons in an engine, a regular heartbeat driving his days forward, and he liked them to run without deviation or wobble.

The odd thing was, even though he knew it was just

something he'd made up to wile away the boredom of his walk, it seemed to be true. When all seven of them were there, he *did* have better days, and the time that he had only seen Grumpy Bike Lady and Old Lady Walker had been a terrible day, *terrible*. Tuesday, however, all seven of them were there, all nodding or greeting him or ignoring him, and all was right with the world and he had a good day. The new project was proving surprisingly easy, and he felt positive and happy.

Wednesday: All seven again, and another good day, making progress, making connections, getting known. Onward and upward, accelerating, the sound of his life running to plan the purr of a well-oiled machine, with Channing driving and steering and in control.

Thursday: Seven, and this morning Smiling Girl smiled very widely at him and looked at him for several heated, physical seconds. Channing smiled back and knew that the time to talk to her was approaching. At work, the project was simple and already he could see its end, see his success, see its conclusion. Life was *fine*.

Friday: Seven, and he finished work early, all tasks completed and the project running to plan. A good day; a good week.

SECOND WEEK

Monday: The Gimp wasn't there, and Dog Man was late, was only a figure in the distance and so Channing didn't get a chance to speak to him, which was odd. Dog Man was the member of the Seven least likely to be absent or delayed. Smiling Girl still smiled at Channing, however, and Old Lady Walker had nodded in her sprightly, no nonsense way, so the journey was still a good one. Smiling Girl's face, in particular, had been open and warm at the station, holding his gaze long enough for it to feel like an invite, something personal and specific and clean. He was a little late arriving at the station, though, so there wasn't time to take Smiling Girl up on her invite before her train came. *Tomorrow,* he thought. *Tomorrow, or if not then, soon.*

Channing arrived at the office to find an email from his manager asking him why he hadn't sent through the first stage of the project implementation plan. Checking back through his emails, panic hollowing his stomach, he found the request buried at the bottom of another email. He had missed it, and the information had been due Friday before he went home. As if to confirm it, his voicemail contained three increasingly irritated messages from his boss, all left after Channing had gone home early on Friday.

Scrambling to fix his error, Channing spent a morning on the phone and email, apologising. Most of the information he needed was available, but it took several hours to pull it into a shape that was both understandable and acceptable, and it was nearly lunchtime before he sent it through. His eyes itched from straining at the computer screen, his ear felt warm and soft from the time it had spent with a phone clamped to it, his throat was dry from the talking and explaining he had had to do. The worst of it was that, whilst he was mostly sure he had rescued the actual situation, he knew he had damaged his reputation with the upper management team. His boss had used the word "disappointed" three times during the course of their morning conversations, which Channing knew was corporate speak for having seriously blotted his copybook. Not a good day.

Tuesday: Dog Man was back in his usual place, and nodded and greeted Channing with a cheery "Hello!" The Gimp was still missing; perhaps he was in hospital being fixed, thought Channing. *I hope it hurts*, he grinned to himself, *teach him to go away and mess my day up!*

Tuesday was better. Smiling Girl was still smiling, the work he had sent through had been received well and he scoured all his emails relating to the new project, making sure that there were no other surprises lurking, no other tasks or deadlines he had missed. After such a chaotic Monday, Tuesday felt like the day Channing regained some sense of equilibrium. The world was righting itself, the engine settling back to rhythm after the previous day's stutter, and all was good.

Wednesday: Turn Face Lady didn't look at him, not even a glance. Of course, she never *really* looked at him, but Channing had always felt some spark with her, something sidelong and sneaked, but this morning for the first time, there was nothing.

"Perhaps she's got a new boyfriend," he muttered out loud, turning as he walked to watch her carry on down the road. "Is that it, Turn Face Lady? New boyfriend so you have to ignore me in case looking at me would bring it all back, would be too much and you'd have to drop him and go back to pining for me? That would explain it." Nonsense, Channing knew. These were just people with whom he had developed some sort of connection simply because he saw them most mornings. It wasn't a serious thing, but all the same he *liked* that Turn Face Lady never quite looked straight at him, almost smiling as she did it, and he felt strange and surprisingly disappointed when she didn't.

No Gimp, but Old Lady Walker still strode energetically and Grumpy Bike Lady was as grumpy as ever and Rockabilly Boy was immaculately groomed, his quiff bending like perfectly formed reeds as he cycled past Channing. Dog Man was cheery, and Smiling Girl smiled as bright as ever, although only through the window of the train as it pulled out because Channing was late again. The project rolled on, Channing contacted people with requests for information and timeframes and completion reports. There was more to it than he'd first thought, but it was still achievable, he knew. He just had to concentrate on it and not be distracted.

Thursday: The Gimp was still gone, and Turn Face Lady still didn't look at him. In fact, she was slightly earlier than normal so Channing only saw her from behind, saw her back and the sway of her buttocks under her long skirt as she walked away, but never got a chance to see her face. Old Lady Walker was slower today, so that he saw her further into his journey than was usual. She looked weary, her shoulders slumped, her head down and her nod to him was tiny, almost imperceptible.

The rest of the commute was uneventful, but the day wasn't good. More work relating to the project came to light that, although it hadn't been part of the original work plan, was given to him to complete. It jeopardised some of his timeframes and deadlines and he had to rework his plan to accommodate it. He also discovered that some of the people he had contacted to arrange for their input were either away or hadn't got the information he needed, so the day ended up as a mess of chasing up and pinning down, of loose ends and false trails.

Friday: Six, and another scrappy, day. The Gimp continued to be AWOL, Turn Face Lady had definitely changed in her attitude to him, Old Lady Walker was still stooped and bent, and even Rockabilly Boy's quiff looked in disarray this morning, one or two strands of oiled hair coming loose as he passed Channing and waving like elegant rats' tails. Only Dog Man, Smiling Girl and Grumpy Bike Lady were as they normally were.

THIRD WEEK

Monday: Turn Face Lady wasn't there. He looked both ways along the street, and even waited for a few moments to see if she showed up, but she was gone. It was stupid, Channing knew, but he wanted to see her. He wanted to see all of them, smiling and grumpy and walking and cycling. *Normal.* A silly superstition, he knew. Not even that really, just a made up thing, his own amusement given a frame on which to hang. They were the markers of his morning, the things that gave him structure. He imagined his life as a smooth, rolling machine and them its parts, and it was unsettling when they were not there, made him feel as though misfires had been introduced into his existence.

Channing looked for them all that morning, but only four of the seven appeared. In addition to Turn Face Lady, the Gimp was still missing as was, for the first time in months, Old Lady Walker. Dog Man was late again although he still nodded at Channing from a few feet away, and Rockabilly

Boy looked positively dishevelled, his hair unknotting in great hanks and sweat shining on his normally smooth brow. Only Grumpy Bike Lady and Smiling Girl were anything like their normal selves, Grumpy Bike Lady's head down and her face flat and grim, and Smiling Girl smiling. Channing stood at the station watching Smiling Girl's train pull away, and wondered what it meant.

Nothing, of course. Nothing. How could it? These were just people he saw, part of a strange little community that he had formed around himself; he didn't even know these people, had simply invented names and personalities for them, almost certainly wouldn't recognise them away from their place on his commuter's path. They had no power over him, weren't an influence on his life, despite whatever little games he played with them in his head to liven up his journey. He was worrying about nothing.

That day, he discovered he had missed another deadline.

Tuesday: Walking in was terrible. Turn Face Lady, The Gimp and Old Lady Walker were still absent and both Rockabilly Boy and Dog Man were wrong, respectively scruffy and late, but it was the worry that made it so bad. Channing had no idea how he had missed this deadline, by which he should have delivered another interim progress report containing implementation data as well as recommendations on developing the next stages of the work. When he checked back through his emails and paperwork, there it was, clear as day—a deadline. He was so sure he'd checked everything, had everything under control, that the engine was running smooth. How could he have missed it?

Channing's boss was furious, and told Channing he would have to answer to an emergency board meeting later in the week, and in the meantime he needed to get the report to them that day. What he ended up sending wasn't good, he knew, but it was at least something, and it might keep him on the project if he was lucky.

At home after the worst day of his working career, Channing thought about what to do next. He was usually so organised, and this missing things, getting things wrong, wasn't like him. He had no idea why life had suddenly shifted towards chaos, but he had to turn it around, and soon. He would have to make sure he completed the next stage of the project on time and to a high standard. That should be easy enough, he thought. Complete concentration, that was all it took.

Wednesday: Rockabilly Boy didn't show up that morning, leaving Channing with only the ever-later Dog Man, Grumpy Bike Lady and Smiling Girl. Dog Man remained silent.

At work he found that the report had been rejected as being poor quality. The email from his boss simply read, *Not acceptable. Be ready to explain yourself at the board tomorrow.*

Thursday: The same three were there, the same four were gone, and the board tore Channing to pieces.

Friday: Dog Man wasn't there and by the end of the day, Channing had been removed from the project management role and had been told by his boss that he could expect a formal review of his performance, and that a warning would almost certainly follow. A bad, bad week. Still, he thought as he walked home, things could only get better. He was still in charge, still driving, still in charge of the machine. He simply needed to regain his control, to adjust and improve. Not easy, for sure, but he could do it.

FOURTH WEEK

Monday: Just Smiling Girl and Grumpy Bike Lady this morning, despite Channing waiting for almost ten minutes in the hope of seeing Dog Man. He knew, just *knew*, it was stupid to think that this minor change to how his mornings fitted together could disrupt his days, his *life*, so much, but he couldn't help it. These seven had been the only constants in his commute besides the land itself, with him through the months of rain and snow and sun and frost and damp and summer storms and low winter sun. They had become a part of his routine, and he didn't like their absence. It made him feel off-kilter, exposed, as though some important element of his life were being stripped away. Parts of the engine were malfunctioning, were falling away from the machine, and he did not understand how it was happening, or why

Channing decided to talk to Smiling Girl. He missed his chance that morning because he had waited too long for Dog Man and had only seen her as she climbed into her train, but tomorrow he thought. Tomorrow. After all, they had spent most of the last year smiling at each other, and he understood now that he had done nothing more because he didn't want to change the contours of his routine, liking their regularity and predictability. Smiling Girl and he smiled at each other, nothing more. Now, of course, his routine was breaking apart anyway, so what did it matter?

At work, Channing opened an email telling him that his formal review was scheduled for Thursday, and that he should bring representation if he had it. He had never joined a union, so he couldn't call on them for help, and he had never really made friends in his office so he would have to go by himself. The notification also told him to bring all relevant documentation, so he spent the day printing emails and collating the hard copy paperwork. In doing so, he found another three small jobs that, within the structure of the overall project, he had also missed doing.

The email also stated that one possible result of his review was the termination of his contract with immediate effect, which startled him. He had thought this might lead to a formal warning, nothing worse. He wondered what he would do if they sacked him; he had spent the last year concentrating on his career to the exclusion of almost everything else, and had no interests outside of work and few people he could call friends. He realised, with a sad little jolt, that he saw Smiling Girl and the others far more often than he saw his parents or sister, more often than he saw the one or two acquaintances with whom he socialised. He spent his time in the evenings watching movies or studying, gaining qualifications that would make him more attractive to his employers. He had invested in himself, he thought bitterly, building a carapace of work around himself, fitting himself into it as tightly as possible, making it as much a part of his identify and his existence as breathing or thinking.

And now, for no reasons that he could discern, it was all tumbling apart.

Tuesday: The fucking Gimp was still gone, Old Lady Walker, Rockabilly Boy, Dog Man, and Turn Face Lady were still fucking gone, and the day was dank and fucking miserable. Channing had slept little, spending most of the night lying awake and thinking of his current predicament, the situation circling in his head like the death of rest and the birth of chaos, and when Grumpy Bike Lady rode into view, he was so glad he almost cried. It was apples in her bag this morning, he saw, green and sallow in the morning's weak light. Her head was down as ever, her short legs pumping down against the pedals. She passed him in a whistle of displaced air and the rattle of waterproof clothing, ignoring him, gloriously, wonderfully, *normally* ignoring him. He turned to watch her go, her back hunched forward and obscuring the handlebars and basket, and he grinned.

Smiling Girl was there as well, sipping one of her infrequent coffees and staring at him through the steam and smiling. *How much invite do you want?* he asked himself. *She's not taking her eyes off you. Talk to her!*

No. Tomorrow, not because he was nervous now but because he simply wanted to enjoy the sense that this at least, that Smiling Girl and Grumpy Bike Lady, were signs of a life still on track, of an engine still functioning, of a machine driving ahead with him at the helm. Tomorrow.

At work, he noticed that his colleagues left a gap around him as he moved through the office, talked to him only when necessary and then only about work. It was as though his current situation, the formal review and his damaged reputation, was infectious and everyone was wary of catching it from him. He tried not to let it worry him and carried on preparing for Thursday, getting his arguments organised in his head. He made himself notes, and as he did so he avoided thinking about how far he had fallen and where he might end up.

Wednesday: As though reflecting his mood, the day dawned grey and sour. Old rain, unspent and lazy, hung in the air like seaweed, draping itself across his clothes and exposed skin as he walked past where Turn Face Lady used to avoid looking at him, past the place where Old Walker Lady had nodded to him and on to where he had passed The Gimp, day in day out since he had started this job. Grumpy Bike Lady struggled past him as usual, Dog Man and Rockabilly Boy were gone and Smiling Girl smiled, wide and open and inviting.

"Hello," said Channing, but under his breath and only when she was on her train. Still, he could not talk to her. It made as little sense as anything else, he supposed, but he had begun to feel that if he broke the routine, it would herald something terrible. "Like what?" he asked himself, trying to analyse it. *Like being on a disciplinary, with a chance of losing your job? Like realising that you have no friends and nothing in your life besides the work that you've just fucked up? Like being a failure?*

Failure. It wasn't something Channing was used to, and it didn't feel good, and he gnawed at it all day as his colleagues shifted about him in a complex dance of avoidance and distance. However he looked at it, he had messed up, had missed things, had *failed*. The result was this situation, this trembling, tottering place he found himself in, where his control was almost gone and he teetered over... what? He didn't know. He gathered his papers, checked his notes, and resigned himself to whatever Thursday would bring.

Thursday: For the first time ever, Grumpy Bike Lady looked up as she drew alongside him, and she smiled. No, she didn't smile, she positively beamed, a twisting of her lips so that they appeared to be stretching right around her head like the features on a melted shop floor mannequin. Channing almost shrieked *Don't! Don't!* but it was too late. The grin wept wide around her head, monstrous, scuttling and leering like a scorpion in amongst the weakening foundations of his life and stabbing at them, setting them to wobble further and further out past their tipping point. There was grit in the engine, the pistons struggling and straining and making a noise like the shriek of a dentist's drill on a tooth.

Channing almost ran the rest of the way to the station, his breath ragged whoops in a chest that felt constricted and inflexible. He emerged on to the platform unable to stop a sob escaping from his mouth when he saw Smiling Girl. She looked around, clearly waiting for him, and when she saw him, she smiled. *She's still here*, he thought. *Still here, still smiling, my beautiful wonderful Smiling Girl, and I still can't talk to you but you're here, you're my constant, you make it safe. Everything will be well, it doesn't matter if Grumpy Bike Lady isn't grumpy, if Dog Man isn't there or Rockabilly Boy starts to dress in clothes smeared with the shit from Dog Man's mongrel, you're still here. It'll be fine if you're still here and still smiling.*

The review board found Channing guilty of gross incompetence and fired him.

Friday: Grumpy Bike Lady didn't show up, and Channing walked the whole journey without seeing anyone he recognised. Of course, he didn't need to make the journey at all, but he had woken that morning hollow and lost without his commute, without work to go to. His body felt like old, deflated meat, discarded and fat and nerveless, and eventually he got dressed and left the house more for something to do than anything else. He walked his route because there was nowhere else to go and besides, it was *his*, marked out in sweat and paces over these previous days and weeks and months and years. He was even ready for Grumpy Bike Lady to smile at him, was intending to send a poisoned grin back, but she wasn't there.

Smiling Girl would be, though. Now, he had no reason not to talk to her. She might even think that his making the journey just to talk to her was romantic; perhaps he could get her train with her and they could get to know each other. After all, he had no other plans.

She was in her usual place, her petite frame almost hidden by the surrounding press of commuters, her long hair tucked behind her ears, and she was looking at him when he arrived at the station. He walked straight to her, looking into her eyes, and said, "Hello."

Smiling Girl didn't respond. "Hello," said Channing again and again she said nothing in return. "Hello," he tried one last time, beginning to wonder if he hadn't misread this whole situation and thinking that if he had, it was about par for the last few weeks' course. His gaze dropped from her eyes, and he took a step back from her. Another step, as though to remove himself from her, to take back the last minutes, but of course, it was too late.

Smiling Girl wasn't smiling; her face was twisted into an expression of wretched, unpleasant hate. He tried to speak again but the words caught in his throat, tiny and dusty and unborn. He swallowed them back down, feeling life tilt and yaw under his feet. Distantly, he heard the sound of something crumbling, crashing, of the machine shaking itself apart, violent and palsied. A new sound came to him, like the discordant clanking and grinding of a distant steam train, spewing dark and coarse clouds from its funnel as it approached and he tried to back away only to find that there was, finally, nowhere to go.

PEEK A BOO

ELLIE WAS IN the kitchen cupboard, amongst the bottles of bleach and cleaners and clothes, and she didn't want to come out.

There was blood on the kitchen floor. Ellie could see it if she pressed her eye close to the tiny gap between the cupboard doors and squinted. She didn't like to do that, though; it made her want to cry again and she knew that if she cried, it might hear her and come looking. At least those other awful noises had finally stopped, the screams, trailing down to pitiful whimpering, that she was sure came from Timothy. She hated hearing Timothy like that, and hated that she was too scared to go and help him. He was her little brother, and she was supposed to look after him, Daddy had told her it was a big sister's job to look after her little brother lots of times.

Mummy had only screamed once and Daddy hadn't made any noise at all except for a little sound like a swallow, as though something had stuck in his throat.

It had started at tea time with a crash from somewhere outside, very loud. It made Mummy jump and Daddy said a rude word, apologising straight away because he knew Mummy didn't like rude words. All four of them left their food (the thick soup made by Mummy that Ellie liked a lot but Timmy didn't like as much) and went out into the garden, and as they did they heard another crash and this time a scream and some shouting. Other doors began to open—Mrs Willow's and Mr and Mrs Griffin's and the Bennett's, all except Mrs Carter because she was deaf and never heard anything. Most of their neighbours were out, looking around and calling to each other over the fences. Ellie's Daddy went to the end of the garden and looked up the street to where the sounds seemed to be coming from. Someone, Mr Bennett she thought, called Daddy, asking if he could see what was happening, and Daddy had said, "No, nothing" and then something moved behind him.

Whatever it was, it appeared out of nowhere, as though the shadows in the sky were swirling and clumping together, dropping to earth to form a huge, moving shape. It seemed to rise behind Daddy as he turned towards it, and then it fell down on him. Daddy had made that funny little noise and then he was gone and Mummy had screamed and someone else had shouted and then the shadow thing leapt across the wall and was running up their garden.

Ellie didn't see what happened next. Mummy pushed her and she started running and Mummy was next to her and then she was gone and Timothy was running past her but then something like grey-brown snakeskin flickered at her side and he was gone as well and Ellie ran. There were more screams and a noise like a huge kettle hissing and then tearing and crunching sounds and Ellie didn't know what to do. She wanted to go back to her Mummy but she was scared, and then Timothy had cried out "Mummy!" like the time he had cut his knee but so much worse and Ellie ran faster and made it into the kitchen as, behind her, something banged up against the kitchen door.

In the zoo once, Ellie had seen a crocodile, but the thing at the door was much bigger and much worse and its teeth were huge and it was looking at *her*. It struggled to get through the doorway because of its size, its shoulders rasping against the sides of the frame and its head jutting into the kitchen, thrashing side to side and Ellie didn't know what to do, so she had run to the only place she could hide.

It must have gone, distracted by something. Ellie didn't know how long she had been in the cupboard. Long enough to hear more shouts, crashes, screams and once a roar that felt like it filled the whole sky and made the earth shake. It sounded as though the thing had gone from the kitchen, was everywhere else in the village at once, going to every house and every person and making the whole place scream. Ellie wondered if God was punishing them for something, but thought that God wouldn't be so cruel as to send the shadow thing. It was too horrible to come from God.

Ellie wanted the toilet, but she dared not move in case it heard her and came back; it might do to her what it had done to Timothy and Mummy and Daddy, so she tried to stay as still and quiet as she did when she played Hide and Seek with Timothy. He was good at that, always finding her and leaping on her and shouting "Peek A Boo!" so that she knew she was caught. Only, she didn't think the thing would shout anything, especially not "Peek A Boo!" It would simply pounce.

The inside of the cupboard smelled sharp and chemical, almost covering the thick, coppery stench that came from outside. The outside smell was like the smell in the toilet when Timothy forgot to flush it, which always made Daddy shout and tell Timmy that he was a "horrible little beast". Thinking of toilets, thinking of Peek A Boo, remembering

Timothy, thinking of how horrible *real* beasts were, made her want to wee even more. She wondered if it was safe to move yet but another terrible roar from outside and a scream that cut off halfway through made her stay still. She clenched her bladder tight, holding her pee in. Despite trying as hard as she could, however, she wasn't able to stop tears from squeezing themselves out of her eyes and rolling down her cheeks. Little hitching noises clasped at her throat and echoed in her mouth. Ellie cried. She wanted her Mummy and Daddy and Timothy.

They did not come. Ellie stayed in the cupboard, in the darkness, and listened as something tore apart her world and all the while, if she looked out from her hiding place, she could see the smears of blood on Mummy's clean kitchen floor. They stretched from the door into the room like fat snakes, dark and coiling. It looked like someone had been trying to write on the floor and Ellie knew her Mummy would hate it if she could see it; she liked things clean and neat and nice, not dirty and horrible and messy.

"Mummy," Ellie whispered out loud, unable to keep the word inside her any longer. It was just too big, filling her chest and pressing down on her tummy and making her feel sick and scared. How could Mummy be gone? How could Daddy be gone? They were going on holiday next month, the four of them, and only yesterday Ellie and her Mummy had been shopping and bought Ellie some new clothes. "Mummy," Ellie said again, crying as she said it.

At first, she thought it was an echo. Just after she said *Mummy* for the second time, the word came back at her, hoarse and wet-sounding. It came again, disintegrating into a bubbly mess as she listened. Ellie shivered when she heard it and wondered if the thing could talk, was repeating what she said to torment her like Ann Gharad sometimes did in the playground at school when she was being particularly mean.

"Mummy," the word came again, and this time it was accompanied by a sort of long scratching, wheezing sound. Ellie held her breath, trying to curl herself into an even smaller ball and retreating further inside the dark cupboard so that the shelf poked into her back and the bottles and sprays jostled against her. It was coming back, the terrible thing that had hurt her Mummy and Daddy and Timothy, coming back for her because somehow it realised that she had been left behind. Through the tiny crack between the doors, she watched as something dark appeared at the bottom of the open doorway, heard the rattling noise again and the word "Mummy," long and twisted and shredded, and then the creature was over the threshold and into the house.

Only, it couldn't be the thing because it was too small and even as she shrieked a little bit, she knew that she recognised the voice saying "Mummy", had heard it every day for the past years, ever since he had learned to talk.

Timothy.

Without thinking, Ellie threw open the cupboard doors, clambered out and went to her brother, not caring now what she knocked over or how much noise she made in her haste. Timothy was very badly hurt, she could see that even before she got to him. He was bent funny, as though someone had twisted the whole bottom half of his body around so that his legs faced sideways instead of to the front. Blood covered him, masking his face and matted in his hair, and there was a big cut across his forehead that had dirt and leaves from the garden stuck in it. He had dragged himself using one arm; the other straggled behind him, the hand at its end sticking out at the oddest angle. Little white nubs that Ellie thought were probably bone poked out from the blood on his wrist.

She knelt beside him, stroking his hair and trying not to cry. *Be brave*, she heard her Daddy say in her head, and thinking that made her want to cry even more but she couldn't because she had to be a big girl and help Timothy because he was her baby brother. So she stroked his hair and didn't mind about the blood that got onto her hands and she told him that it was going to be alright, he was going to be okay.

When he felt her hand on his head, Timothy began to make awful little mewling sounds and he wouldn't stop even when she tried to tell him to shush, because it might hear him and come back. He was crying as well, she saw, and saying "Mummy" and "Daddy" and "Ellie" in the middle of all the mewling and she wanted so much for him to be quiet and he wouldn't so she bent down low over him, hoping that she could hug him and make him feel better and that's when she felt the gentle waft of air across her back.

It wasn't like a breeze, because it was too warm and it smelled of dirt and meat, and Ellie knew what it was. She stood and turned at the same time, putting herself between her brother and the thing crouching on the other side of the doorway. Blood, glittering like fire, dripped from its mouth, ruby droplets spattering across the floor as it took a step forward and pushed its head into the room. Timothy cried out, fearful, but Ellie said out loud, "Don't worry, I'll look after you" and the thing's jaw opened wide, so impossibly wide, and in the depths of its throat Ellie saw glints like a thousand stars, winking and cold.

"Go away," Ellie said as clearly as she could. "Leave my brother and me alone."

The creature lunged forward, forcing itself into the room, its mouth gaping. Constellations closed about Ellie in a red, savage wave and then she was flying, borne along by Timothy's screams and the sound of bones cracking.

There's a wild boar in the wood,
He'll eat your flesh and he'll drink your blood
Down in the grove where the flowers grow
and the green leaves fall all around

Bold Sir Rylas, trad.

COEL COETH

A ND THE STREETS were full of monsters.

Holding Allie's hand, Harding walked the lanes and sidewalks of the place of her birth and watched as children of all ages went from house to house and demanded treats. He saw spiders and creepy clowns holding balloons and aliens, several children with the bobbing insectile antennae on springs that he'd called 'deeley boppers' when he was young, a brace of witches, a veritable army of zombies and one small girl made to look like a drowned woman. She had limp, wet hair, painted blackness around her mouth and eyes and her skin blanched down to a fishbelly pale, a costume that seemed to Harding somehow both elegant and sad and yet terribly adult and inappropriate. They carried baskets and bags of sweets, these monsters, giggling and chewing as they walked, adults shepherding the younger beasts, leading gaggles of them in crocodiles across the roads and along pavements.

Older children ran unsupervised, their costumes more perfunctory, masks over heads but no attempt at costumes except for the teen uniform of hoodies and jeans. Mostly they

165

ignored everyone but their own age group, although one teenage boy did run up to Harding and Allie wearing a mask fashioned into the face of an old man and rubber finger extensions with ragged, long nails that he waved at their faces while cackling evilly. Given that the rubber fingers were filthy and that the worst threat the boy could make was to offer to prepare a meal whilst wearing them, Harding was going to shoo him away without reward but seeing the look of enjoyment on Allie's face he dug out a handful of chocolates from his pocket and handed them over. How Allie looked at him when he did it was reward enough, a treat he hoped to sample later.

They strolled through Halloween, Harding and Allie, and enjoyed each other and the world around them.

Later, as the streets started to empty, Harding assumed they'd be going back to Allie's parents' house, where they were staying for a long weekend. He hoped to be able to pull Allie into a pub or restaurant on the way back, to spend time with her somewhere warm and snug, huddled into a corner head next to her head so that he could smell her closeness and tell her he loved her, but instead she pulled him to the village's outskirts and started up into the hills.

"Where are we going?" he asked as she walked ahead of him, one hand holding his hand as though needing to pull him. He didn't really mind the change of plans or where they were going, to be honest; just being with her was enough. A hillside somewhere unpronounceable in Wales was as good as anywhere else, and better than most because they were alone except for each other. In the evening's moonlit darkness the curve of her buttocks in tight denim and the sweep of her thigh were magnificent to behold, and when she turned back the light caught in her smile and made it something beyond beautiful, something endless and alive and turned her eyes into glimmering silver pools that he felt he could let himself fall into and willingly drown in.

Towards the top of the hill Allie pulled Harding off the path and towards a copse of old trees whose trunks were gnarled and twisted, the weight of their crowning leaves and branches pulling them down into crone shapes. In amongst the trees the air was warmer, smelled of moss and clean, damp earth and something else, something sharper that reminded Harding of winter nights from his childhood. It was the smell of bonfires, and it increased as they pushed further into the darkness. They slowed, Allie still ahead, feeling with their feet for roots and other obstructions, stepping over and around until at last they came to a clearing in which a fire burned.

It filled most of the space before them, a circle of heavy stones in whose centre a mass of wood had been reduced to glowing orange embers. The heat of it was heavy and damp, made Harding sweat and forced him to open his coat, the smell of it thick with sap and leaf and ash. Apart from the fire, the clearing was empty.

Well, almost empty. There was a cairn of small stones to one side of the fire. Allie let go of Harding's hand and went to it, picking up two stones and handing him one. From a pocket in her jacket she took a sharpie and wrote something on the stone then turned and threw it into the fire. When she turned back to him, she was smiling but the smile looked old, somehow, and tinged with something he couldn't identify. Melancholy? Sadness? Something vaster than her and him, anyway. A recognition of their smallness against the walls of the universe. She was holding the pen out to him and he took it saying, "What am I supposed to do with this?"

"Write a prayer on the stone and throw it into the fire."

"Allie, I'm not religious, you know that."

"It doesn't matter. This is *coel coeth*, and it's a tradition we have. It's a Welsh thing, I think. Some places do it on Bonfire night and I think some do it on the winter solstice but here we've always done it on Halloween," and she dropped her head so that her chin was against her neck and her eyes were peering out at him from suddenly shadowed brows and intoned hollowly, "when the barriers between this world and the others are at their thinnest."

She lifted her head again and her eyes were bright again and she was smiling. "Now, city boy, you write your heart's desire on the stone, a prayer or a wish or whatever, and you throw it into the fire and God, or the universe or our own will or the fairy folk or whoever it is that controls these things, decides if it's a good wish, if you're worthy enough, and if you are the whatever makes it come true."

"Really?"

"Really."

"Who lights the fire?" he asked, intrigued, thinking about what to write. What did he want, really? What did he want his life to be? What didn't he already have? What did he need?

"No one knows," Allie replied, still smiling but now it was broader, happier, the smile of someone enjoying herself. Suddenly, Harding thought he might be being taken for a ride and lowered stone and pen.

"Allie, how can you not know? Someone must come up here to get the fire pit ready, bring the wood and light it, and they must do it early so that it's down to embers for this time of night. Someone must put the stones in a pile for people to use."

"Maybe they do, but I don't know who it is and no one ever talks about it. And not everyone comes up here, only people who want something and there's never anyone else here when you come up and you never see anyone on the way to or from the clearing. It's how it's always been. Now, write your prayer or wish."

Harding thought for another moment then wrote across the stone's rough surface, throwing it into the fire by Allie's stone when he had finished. "Now what?" he asked.

"We wait a few minutes," Allie replied. "Be thankful you didn't have to do this a few years ago. When I was a kid we had to write on the stones with the burned end of a stick in ash, so your prayers or wishes or whatever had to be really short. We'd just have to write things like 'Money' or 'Love'! Once, I came up and wrote 'Sex' on a stone, can you believe it? Just that, just 'Sex' and it took ten minutes to get it legible. Sharpies have made things easier, and a damn sight more eloquent."

"Did it ever work?"

"Well, I have sex with you, don't I?" she asked and he could hear the tease and salacious grin in her voice even though he couldn't see her face because she was leaning towards the fire, a mere silhouette against the wavering orange heat.

"What are you doing?"

"Getting the stones," she said, and he saw she was using a stick to roll the stones to the edge of the pit and then up over the surround. When they fell to the ground, two glowing eggs of fire, she used the stick to push them into the earth where they made the damp mud steam gently and crackle as it dried. "While we're waiting for them to cool, was there something you wanted to ask me?"

"Oh," he said, and then, "do you want to go for a drink on the way back?" through a suddenly dry mouth.

"The other question," she said and stepped close to him so that she was pressed against him, head tilted back and looking up to him, the heat of her greater than the heat of the fire. Her lips parted slightly as she looked at him and her tongue traced across the edge of her upper teeth. "Well?"

Harding leaned down so that his mouth was just over hers and, very quietly and on an exhalation so that his breath passed into her, said, "Will you marry me?"

"Yes," she replied and they kissed then and for a glorious moment they were the only things in the universe, in all of time and space there was just them and the kiss and the future they had just decided to share, and when they broke the kiss the moment stayed in the air around them and settled into Harding's skin like smoke, like the tattoo of a promise.

Later, after he and Allie had had not just a drink but a meal to celebrate, and had told her parents who made them have another drink, they went up to the room they shared and started to undress. They were down to their underwear when Allie said, "Wait, there's another thing we have to do!"

"What?"

"Come with me," she said, digging something from her coat pocket and pulling him from the room into the hallway. Uncomfortably aware of his near-nudity he tried to resist but she was inexorable, leading him into the bathroom. She turned on one of the taps so that water flowed into the sink and then held up the two stones, now cool and ashy and muddy. Gesturing at him to hold his hand out, she dropped one into his upturned palm and said, "That's yours."

"How do you know?"

"Just do. Now, you have to wash it." So saying, she held her stone under running water, rinsing it clean and then held it up before him again, showing him that its surface was unmarked. No trace of the writing remained. "The universe has agreed, or God has answered my prayer, or granted my wish. Whatever, I'm good. Now you."

Harding washed his stone and found it also unblemished. "Looks like I lucked out too," he said and grinned at her. "Now, shall I take you to bed?"

'Yes, please," she said, "and make it good, but keep it quiet. I don't want my parents to hear."

"Of course," he said and took her back to the bedroom and they were quiet and it was as good as it had ever been between them and just at the moment he lost himself inside her he thought, *She's my fiancée, we'll be together forever and this is how life will be* and it was the finest thought he'd ever had. The next morning they lay in, both having taken time off work so that their visit to Wales could be a relaxed one. He woke before her and watched her for a time, enjoying the steady rise of her chest and the way her face slackened in rest, the faint lines of concentration that usually creased her forehead smoothed away to nothing. She was beautiful, he'd always known that, but now her beauty seemed enhanced by the love he felt for and from her, turning her into something that seemed almost inhuman in its glory. *I hope all people in love feel like this,* he thought, smiling inside at his soppiness even whilst he enjoyed it.

Allie mumbled something and moved slightly, and that was when the spider scurried up onto her face, across her cheek and stopped, nestling into the curve made between the top of her nose and the arc of her eyebrows.

It seemed huge, its abdomen hairy and bulbous, its legs arched across her cheeks, its feet on her forehead and lower face, and its eyes glittered with reflections that looked as deep and endless as stars circling distant galaxies. It had fangs, curved scythes jutting from a black maw below those eyes, and it seemed to be looking at him, recognising him, knowing him. Harding, too stunned to make a sound, jerked back and the jerk woke Allie up. Her eyes opened, peering at the spider's underside. She swore distractedly and raised a hand up, and before he could stop her she knocked the creature away. It fell back, disappearing behind her as she rolled to face him.

"Jesus!" he finally managed to gasp and pulled her towards him.

"Frisky," she said, "but let me wake up first. It's too early, you haven't even brought me a cup of tea in bed yet."

"There was a spider, it crawled up on your face," he said, looking warily behind her and trying to see the bastard thing. "It was huge, looked like a fucking tarantula."

"Was that what it was? Oh well. We're in Wales, you get used to nature not respecting your boundaries, but a tarantula? I don't think so. It was probably just a wolf spider, they get pretty big and this time of year they come inside looking for a mate, trying to get in a last desperate shag before the winter kills them. We're used to them out here in the country, but they obviously still scare you soft city dwellers. Tarantula indeed! Now, where's my tea?"

Was that it, he wondered as he made them drinks, padding around her parents' warm kitchen, *was I scared by a big house spider. I mean, do they grow that large? Was it that large, or did I just blow it up into something it wasn't because I'm not used to them?*

They had tea in bed and then made love again, enjoying the lack of responsibility, and then went downstairs for breakfast where Allie told her parents about the incident. Eventually, because Allie didn't seem bothered and her parents laughed with her when she told them and all three took to calling the creature 'Harding's Tarantula', he joined in the laughter and accepted that he simply wasn't used to country living. Still, when they were back in the room dressing he made sure that he jerked the duvet on the bed back and banged around the room loudly to scare the spider away. 'Harding's Tarantula' it might be, joke it might be, but he didn't want to see it again.

He hadn't bought a ring because he hadn't planned his proposal so they went shopping that morning and Harding spent a frightening portion of his monthly salary on a delicate diamond engagement ring, and then they went for a drink. They found a pub that was quiet and shadowed and ordered food and then Allie left Harding to go to the lavatory. Sitting in a comfortable seat in a booth, he started to think forward. Marriage. He tasted the word, liking the feel of it in his mouth, liking the texture and depth of it. He wondered about their future, about what it would contain. They didn't live together yet, had never even discussed co-habitation or children, all that was to come, and he found himself looking forward to it all, no matter what it ended up looking like. He was just beginning to grasp the enormity, the *rightness*, of what they had chosen to do when the shadows at the base of the bar moved.

The pub wasn't full but there were people in it, other diners, and their legs and the chairs and tables blocked the movement after he first saw it, crowding it out in shuffles and strips, but then it came again. Something was slipping along the floor in the space below the rail that ran along the bar at just above floor level for drinkers to put their feet on. The something was long and low, gliding along serenely among the feet and legs, apparently undisturbed by the people around it.

Was it a dog? A rat? *Jesus*, Harding thought, *is that a rat?*

No. It moved too smoothly, like a fast-flowing spill of water. It was long, too, too long to be a rat, stretching two or three feet although he still couldn't make it out. It was as though some darker patch had displaced the usual shadows, was cutting through them below the brass rail, moving along silently, heading deeper into the pub with some purpose only it knew.

Coming closer.

At the corner of the bar, instead of following it around, the shape instead turned and started out across the open floor towards him. No one else seemed to react, the people at the tables between him and it or the people at the bar ordering, collecting drinks, none of them saw it and they should, they *should,* because it was a thing that shouldn't have been, *couldn't* have been, because now Harding could see it clearly.

It looked like a trilobite, broad and squat, its segmented black carapace gleaming dully, hundreds of legs just visible around its edge scuttling it across the expanse of scuffed wooden boards. Antennae on the front of what Harding had to assume was its head dipped and swayed as it came, feeling out its route. Harding wanted to move but found he couldn't; the sheer oddness of seeing the thing had locked him in place. Was it a joke? A dog or cat in a costume, some expensive adult child's Halloween toy like the drones that he saw people fly sometimes? An elaborate trick?

The thing stopped. Its front end reared up, flexing back, segment of its armoured hide disappearing under segment as it rose, revealing on its underside a downturn sickle mouth full of tiny, bitter teeth. Like the spider, it seemed to be looking directly at Harding and still no one else reacted to it, no one else saw it and oh Christ what was it, what was it this thing scuttling impossibly across the floor? Harding wanted to scream, wanted to run but movement seemed lost to him, as though the strings between his brain and muscles had been cut. It hissed then, mouth opening wider and a sound emerging like air escaping from a punctured throat, shrill and wet.

It dropped and moved again, arrowing at him. When it reached the table closest to Harding it vanished under it, losing itself among the feet of the diners seated there. Its absence broke whatever spell had been holding him and Harding shuddered, letting out a ragged breath. He snapped his feet up off the floor, hearing a tiny wail emerge from his mouth, all the noise he could make, and watched at the point where he expected the thing to emerge.

Nothing.

After a moment, Harding ran a shaking hand over his face. Adrenaline flooded his system and he began to shake, the wail turning into a series of broken hitches, aware that the people nearest to him were looking at him curiously and then Allie's hand was on his shoulder and she was sitting beside him and saying, "What? What's wrong? Sweetie?"

When he'd caught his breath back, snatching it out of the air in long gasps, Harding managed to calm and speak. "Is there something under the table?"

"Our table?" asked Allie, looking down.

"No, that one?" said Harding, pointing, ignoring the people sitting at the table who were now staring openly at him.

Allie bent, peering under the table, before sitting up. "There's nothing there except feet and legs and dust," she said quietly. "Babe, what's wrong?"

"I saw..." he said before trailing off. What? What had he seen? An insect the size of a child moving like an oilslick across the floor. "I don't know."

"You don't know?"

"No. I mean, I saw something but I don't know if it was there, or if I saw it right. I can't have done, I don't think."

"You mean you hallucinated it?" asked Allie and ran her hand along his arm. "Has it happened before?"

"No. I mean—" and there was a thump as the waitress set their food dishes down, ending the conversation.

Food, even though Harding wasn't hungry any more, seemed to ground him, anchoring him back into this reality where Allie was his wife-to-be and the worst thing on the bar floor was mud from the hillwalkers' boots, and by the time they'd finished the insect seemed like a memory of a thing half-seen through screens of glass and muslin, something unreal. Allie looked at him all the time they were eating, and when they finished said, "If you're having second thoughts you can just say. I don't want you to do anything you don't want, and I don't want the thought of marrying me making you hallucinate." She was smiling as she spoke but her voice and eyes were serious.

"What? No," he said, "God, Allie, marrying you will be the best thing I'll ever do. I just had a moment. Not about you," he added hastily, seeing the look on her face.

"A moment?"

"Let's go outside and walk," he said, "and I'll tell you." And he did, everything from the spider again and how large it had seemed to the insect scurrying at him across the floor. When he had finished, Allie was silent for a minute before she spoke.

"And it's not some elaborate ploy to disentangle yourself from me?"

"No. God, no."

"Well, we've both been working hard," she said, and it was true, they had. They'd met a few months ago whilst working in a coffee shop and both were working other jobs, Harding as an office cleaner and Allie in a restaurant in the evenings. "Maybe the stress of it's got a bit much? Plus, you're a city boy at heart, maybe the country air has affected your brain?"

"Maybe," he said and realised he was smiling because that was what Allie could do for him, make him smile no matter what.

"Don't go insane, sweetie," Allie said. "Not yet, anyway. Let's have a few sane years, shall we?"

"If you insist," said Harding, still smiling, and as they walked he tried not to think about spiders and insects the shape of teardrops with mouths like downturned screams.

In the middle of the night, Harding woke because his legs and arms ached. It was a shooting, wavering pain that seemed to pulse out from his elbows and knees to fill his skin like hot water.

He rolled out of bed, careful not to wake Allie or make a noise that might disturb her parents. Walking eased the pain a little and he stepped quietly around the room, going to the end of the bed and back again and waving and bending his arms slowly. His joints popped as he moved, the noise reminding him of his father and grandfather, of the noises of their aging. He wondered if he was getting old, felt the dull ache still festering in his muscles, and thought that he probably was.

Finally Harding stopped by the window. Carefully, so as not to let any light fall on Allie and disturb her, he parted the curtains and peered out at the street beyond. Allie's parents lived at the foot of one of the hills, not the one that the fire they had cast their wishes into had been on but still a significant lump of landscape. It blocked the night beyond it, a black mass between Harding and the rest of the world, its flank furred with trees and foliage just visible in the glow of the lights from the street. *I could get used to this,* Harding thought, *no cars or distant sirens, no half-eaten kebabs left on the doorstep or pissed clubbers puking and screaming. Maybe we should end up somewhere like this, where there's peace and space and we can breathe.* Harding pressed his forehead against the glass, liking its coolness, letting his gaze soften, looking not outside but in, thinking nothing but future thoughts.

There were people in the trees at the bottom of the slope.

They were just beyond the treeline, perhaps forty or fifty yards past the wire fence that separated the hill from the street, and Harding knew immediately that they weren't walkers or late night revellers, they belonged to the place that the insect and the spider belonged to because yes the spider belonged there too, he knew that now. Something in his world had fallen off-kilter, and the figures were the latest manifestation of it, of his mental illness or whatever it was. Three of them, hunched and cowled, they moved through the trees, seeming to dance and jig yet never revealing themselves except for the flash of something pale, a skinny wrist or gnarled hand, as they threw their arms up and their robes fell back.

Robes? Yes, robes, black robes that hung to their feet, robes with hoods that rose to jagged points behind their heads and formed ovals of darkness where their faces should be, robes that flailed and flapped, witches' robes. They were witches, the figures, witches taken from some child's fairy tale, clichéd and nonsensical but real enough because he could see that they were kicking grass up, flicking it from their feet and out towards the road. Harding started to laugh at the absurdity of it, at the terror of it, of these three witches who were undoubtedly crones as well under those robes dancing along the outskirts of Welsh suburban peace.

"What's wrong?" asked Allie from behind him and Harding laughed harder, trying to stay silent, tears leaking from the corners of his eyes, and gestured her to him. He heard her rise and the sound of her footfalls, gentle against the carpet, and then she was pressing against him.

"I'm going insane," he said through the laughter and tears. "I'm sorry, I tried to wait a few years but clearly I failed. I'm going mad."

"Really?" asked Allie, and then said, "I'm not so sure, sweetie, because if you think you're mad because you can see three prancing jokers in the trees then I must be going mad too."

It took a second for what Allie had said to sink in, and then Harding said, "You can see them?"

"Three of them," replied Allie, "dancing. They aren't coming out into the light but I know they're there."

"Yes! Yes!" said Harding, "Dancing! And there was an insect before!"

"Well, let's not go too far," said Allie, moving away from him. He continued to watch the figures as a series of rustlings and shufflings came from behind him. Out in the trees, the figures capered.

"Here," said Allie, coming back to Harding's side and handing him his jeans and a jumper. "Let's go and see what's going on."

The woods were dark. *Isn't that the start of a poem, or story*, Harding thought? *Isn't it the start of most fairy tales, the woods are dark and the path through them long and hazardous, and once upon a time there was a lost child or a betrayed adult?* Which role was he here, stumbling amongst the trees following Allie, following the noises, her hand in his as ever? Child or adult?

Something flashed ahead of him, pale and sickly in the darkness, crablike. A hand? An upturned face, cowl falling back as the dance grew more frenzied?

Again, more of the pale flashes now, hands and faces, yes, all of them, the three figures solidifying out of the gloom, their dance a jumbled and capering thing visible in the light

179

from the stars and the moon, the gleam outlining the shadows of robes as knees kicked up high and arms rose and fell, as heads rolled back to face the sky and then dropped again and as they came closer Harding realised that there was chanting, or singing, some low and sonorous sound that gave the night a voice.

"Hey," called Allie, lifting the small torch she'd brought with her and sending the beam at the three figures.

"He arrives," called back a hoarse, cackling voice and the three figures stopped and the glade they were in was suddenly full of light, more light than the torch could create, blazing light that etched them with hard edges and birthed long, reaching shadows. Each of the three turned to face Harding and Allie and then raised an arm, pointing at them. The one in the centre threw their head back, flicking the hood away, to reveal a pallid face framed by straggling hair, the eyes sunken and the nose hooked and bony. It was a woman, and when she opened her mouth her teeth were weathered, blackened tombstone stumps. She wailed, and the other two joined in, pointing directly at Harding now, and the sound was full of threat.

"Who the fuck are you?" asked Allie, stepping forward, ignoring the brightness of the light.

"We are us," said the woman, somehow wailing the words, elongating each one so that it stretched and yawed from her mouth, "and we come for him."

The fingers were extended now, clawed and filthy nails itching the air between them and Harding.

"Me?" he said. "Me? What have I done?"

"You called," the woman said again and then the light blinked out, and in the dizzying flash of afterimage, the figures turned and darted away, disappearing into the trees and flowing from sight. On the ground, impaled with pins, lay a doll that looked vaguely like Harding, the only evidence they had ever been there.

Later Harding and Allie sat in her parents' kitchen drinking coffee, the doll on Harding's knee. Allie had pulled the pins from it and Harding's aches had immediately dissipated. They looked at each other for a long time before Allie said it.

"They looked like witches to you?"

"Yes," said Harding, thankful that she'd brought it up, that she'd seen it too.

"How do you know?"

"How do I know what?"

"That they were witches?"

Harding opened his mouth to answer and then closed it again. How *had* he known? He thought about it, and then said, framing it halfway between a question and a statement, "Because they looked like witches?"

"How, though? How did they look like witches?"

"Because they looked like witches are supposed to look. They had ragged robes, and bare feet, and their hair was messy. The one whose face we saw was ugly and had a hooked nose."

"And warts."

"And warts," he agreed.

"But that's odd, isn't it? Because witches aren't like that, not in real life, are they? At least, I can't imagine they are. I mean, have you ever met anyone who looked like that? Those three, they were like the clichés of witches, what witches are supposed to look like," Allie said, "based on all the fairy tales and Disney films and whatever. It's like they were playing at being witches. And the doll is like a cliché of what witches do."

"Yeah," said Harding because Allie was right, they'd looked like how you'd describe witches if you were asked about them, acted how they'd act if you made up a witch for a story, "so they were joking? Being stupid?"

"No," said Allie. "No, I don't think they were, and that's what doesn't make sense. People dressed as clichéd witches, and threatening you. Do you think it was actually you they wanted? They can't, can they? I mean, they presumably picked you at random because you were the first person to come along?"

Harding, looking at the doll looking back at him from his knee, said nothing.

Then the dead came.

It was their last full day with Allie's parents and they had a meal planned for that night—Harding was cooking something spicy, he had told them, but had not yet decided what to actually cook—and they were walking to the local shop to browse ingredients for him to make a final decision. The shop was small and inspiration sadly lacking so Harding had come to the conclusion that a basic curry might be best when he happened to glance at the front of the store and out through the windows to the street beyond.

There was a zombie shuffling along the other side of the glass.

It was a man, old, his hair dragging in wisps over a near-bald, greying scalp. His mouth was open, pulled down at the corners as though the man had had a catastrophic stroke that had somehow plucked the muscles from his lips so that they drooped revealing yellowing, dry teeth. Harding watched, wondering if it was someone late for Halloween, or a prank was being played on someone, as the man, the zombie, lurched forward, one leg dragging. He swung a shoulder sideways, bumped against the shop window and slid along it, leaving a smear that looked as dry as mothdust. When it, when *he*, reached the shop doorway, the man turned and looked in the store, his eyes glazed and pale. His head jerked as he stared, twitching like some palsied marionette, until his gaze fell on Harding.

The dead man smiled. It was a terrible thing, a rictus straining at the edges not to become a grotesquery, lips peeling back and splitting as the smile stretched across the dead man's face. Dust, or something like it, spilled from his mouth, and then he moved again.

He sloped into the shop, arms rising, one shoulder lower than the other, tongue lolling from its twisting mouth. It never took its gaze off Harding as it shuffled along the first aisle, bumping into other shoppers who didn't seem to notice, moving around the zombie, stepping out of its way and then carrying on their browsing and taking items from the shelves. Harding, still unsure of what was happening, tapped Allie on the shoulder, drawing her attention from the various sauces that they had moments before been trying to choose between.

"Can you see that?" Harding asked her, nodding at the man who had now reached the end of the their aisle and was starting to shuffle determinedly along it. He bumped into a display of cans and they fell, rolling across the floor. A shop assistant came and started picking them up, ignoring the shambling thing just ahead of him.

"Yes," said Allie, her voice small.

"Good," said Harding, "it's not just me then. Is it real?"

"Yes," said Allie, not hesitating. "It's a dead man. A zombie."

"Jesus. What do we do?"

Allie took Harding's hand and led him to the far end of the aisle, past shelves of wine and beer, the zombie still plodding after them, and went into the next aisle. This one led back down to the shop's door and they walked fast along it, still holding hands, still hearing the sounds the zombie made, the low moans and the drag of its feet as it shuffled along. They reached the door and pushed past people to get through it, going out into the street and the sunlight beyond. Harding went along the front of the shop so that he could see up the aisle they had been in.

The zombie had gone.

Shoppers picked items, the assistant was still restacking the spilled cans, the basket they had abandoned was still on the floor at the end of the aisle, but the dead man was gone.

"What's happening?" asked Harding. "Am I going mad? Are you?"

There was another groan, like thunder collapsing against distant hills, and when they turned another zombie, a woman this time and fresher so that blood still dribbled from a wound in her scalp and spilled from the dragging intestine dripping from the tear in her belly, was staggering along the street towards them. As they watched her feet became tangled in her own guts and she fell, hitting the ground hard. After a second, her head came up and she stared at Harding and then moaned again and started to pull herself along the ground towards him.

"Come on," said Allie and pulled Harding again, leading him away from the crawling woman back towards her parents' home. As they went, walking quickly but never quite breaking into a run, she said, "You aren't mad because if you were I wouldn't have seen it but I did, just like the witches last night, and I did see them and I did see the two zombies just now. There's something odd going on, man of mine."

"Odd," echoed Harding, marvelling at how inadequate a word that was to describe these last few days.

"Odd," repeated Allie firmly, "but we'll work out what it is, this odd thing, and we'll sort it. After all, I've only just got my wish and got you to ask me to marry you and I'm not having anything mess it up now, not zombies that apparently only we can see or bugs, not *anything*."

Harding stopped. Allie pulled on his hand again but this time he didn't move, still except for his lips which were pacing out words, framing an idea that seemed absurd yet oddly right. "Allie," he said, "what did you wish for on Halloween night?"

"What?"

"What did you wish for? Up at the fire? In that coelacanth thing?"

"Coel Coeth," Allie said, giggling and he loved her then more than he ever had, felt a wash of emotion so powerful it was almost breathtaking because she could still laugh despite the dead and the women in the trees and the insect that she hadn't seen but that she believed he had seen, could still laugh and he knew he needed her by his side forever because if she could laugh, he could laugh, and if they could laugh then everything would be okay. "I wished for you. For you and me to be together until the very end."

"Just that?"

"What more do I need?"

Harding thought, still chewing an idea, trying to mulch it down to something manageable, something understandable. Allie had wished for him and he'd proposed that night, something he'd been planning to do anyway but hadn't it suddenly felt right, suddenly felt more than right after she had thrown the pebble into the fire? Yes, yes it had suddenly been right, the rightest thing ever.

And what had he written?

"Allie," he said, "I think I know what's happening. I think. It's the coel coeth thing, what I wrote and what the fire granted."

"But that's just a silly tradition, it's not real."

"Isn't it? Your wish came true, didn't it? I wrote a wish and I think it's been granted."

"Well, what did you wish for?"

"We'd had such a lovely day, been together, and it had been so much fun, and I'd not left your side all day and I didn't want that to stop."

"Babe, what did you write?"

"I asked for the day not to stop. Allie, I asked for Halloween with you to never end."

The climb felt harder this time, the way steeper and the ground more uneven.

They had gone back to Allie's parents' home first, the journey thankfully uneventful. No more of the dead appeared although Harding thought he saw shadows massing in an alleyway and once Allie had jumped at something she had seen but he had not, dismissing his querying look with a wave of her hand and a smile that looked distinctly shaky. At the house, they had gone to the bedroom and drawn the curtains so that the street outside and anything it contained could not see them, made coffees and sat and talked.

It made no sense.

It made exact sense, because all the things Harding had seen on Halloween night he had seen since, hadn't he, but made into an odd reality. The spider on Allie's face, the insect in the pub and then the dead, that staple of modern Halloween, all pasty faced and deep-eyed and mangled. Had there been something else he had seen? He couldn't remember despite Allie's questions. "Forewarned is forearmed," she told him, "if we're going to get through this with no more surprises.

"How do we get through it," Harding asked, "how do we stop it?"

Harding's first plan was to get in the car and drive, back to the city and to lights and noise and kebabs spilled on the street and clubs that let out at 5 in the morning like vomiting whales, but Allie argued against it. "It's bad enough here," she said, "but imagine if it comes with us. Imagine trying to track zombies though rush hour or bugs on the northern line on a Saturday night."

The next plan was to ignore it. This was Allie's idea, because as she said, nothing had actually harmed either of them. "Not yet," Harding had said, remembering the way the insect had hissed at him and the way both of the dead had reached out for him. They hadn't hurt them because, what, they hadn't reached him? Because this thing, whatever it was, was building up, creating a reality in which it came closer and closer before finally closing with him and taking hold? And what then? Eaten by an insect, or a zombie, Allie dead through the venomous bite of some ghastly spider? No. Ignoring it was not an option Harding liked.

"Can we fight it?" asked Harding.

"What, kill the zombies or insects? Well, if no one else can see them you'd look like you were attacking the air, you'd be locked up and then you'd be easier for it to get. Or you'd be attacking a normal person who just looks like a zombie, and you'd be arrested. No, that's not the way. I wonder if we're looking at this wrong?"

"In what way?"

"Well, maybe the solution is in the origin. I mean, why? Why you?"

"I don't know," said Harding truthfully. He wasn't, he didn't think, a bad man. He tried to live a good life, he didn't hurt people, he tried to treat people they way he wanted to be treated. Shit, he even gave to charity. "I'm a decent man, I think."

"You are, you're my good man," said Allie, taking his hand. "So. Pissed off any old welsh gods recently? Missed an appointment with any wicker men?"

"Not to my knowledge," he replied, grinning despite everything, "unless you can piss off the old ones by doing something innocent?"

"Oh, I'll bet you can piss off the old ones in any number of ways," said Allie. "You can probably do it just by breathing in an odd pitch on the wrong day of the week, or walking in the wrong direction over an old grave or something. Well, if you can't think of anything, we'll have to ask the fire, won't we?"

"The fire?"

"The fire. It started this nonsense, it can help us end it."

It was a long journey, moving along tiny streets, heads down, avoiding the rambling, staggering dead. The streets were filling with them now, all of them seeming to move their heads in lazy swivels, trying, Harding assumed, to catch sight of him. Thankfully, they seemed as dense and lifeless as the zombies in the bad movies he and Allie sometimes watched, and as slow moving, and none had a chance to do more than glance at them before they were passed and gone. At one point a knotted mass of the dead blocked the street ahead of them but Allie knew an alleyway that connected to a narrow passage along the side of two houses and they avoided them without too much difficulty.

There was another insect at the end of the passage, and this time Allie saw it. The two of them froze as it scuttled by, not looking in their direction, its body low and segmented, long antennae bobbing before it as though tasting the pavement. It hissed as it went, a long, stretched sound like the run-out groove noise of the singles of Harding's teenage years. "They're not looking very hard for you," whispered Allie, "are they?"

"No," said Harding, feeling oddly guilty, as though it was his fault.

"It's like the purpose is in the appearance, not in the catching of you, it doesn't make sense. Let's go," said Allie after another moment when nothing had appeared in the exit from the passage. They went, scurrying in the opposite direction to the insect, reaching the wooded slope without further incident.

And the hill was steep.

The path to the clearing that the fire had been in was covered, the tree branches forming an interlocked ceiling above Harding and Allie, the trunks to either side of them seeming to grow thicker and denser the further they went. Harding could feel the effort in his calves and thighs, and the air was full of the sound of things crackling and treading around them. He saw shadows moving in the peripheries of his vision, saw the dead closing in and spiders dropping from above them, grotesque bodies dangling from silken thread, fangs pregnant and dripping with venom, saw ripples in the earth's covering of rotting leaves shifting and moving as buried insects flowed through the dankness like mouthed torpedoes yet when he looked around they were gone and the leaves dripped with nothing more than old rain and the earth was humped with nothing more threatening than twisted roots and stems. Harding tried to keep his eyes down, looking at nothing but his feet, but still the world was clustered with threatening shadows as all the Halloween monsters crept closer and closer until he thought he would burst, thought he would scream and maybe this was the point, maybe the point was to drive him mad rather than have him eaten by corpses or torn apart by impossible creatures, and then he was screaming, aching and screaming inside his closed mouth and Allie was holding his hand and saying, "It's okay, honey, it's okay. We're here."

The glade was dark, the fire almost burned to nothing now but there was still heat here, heat and the dull orange glimmer of embers in the centre of the pit. "If it's Halloween every day, the fire has to burn," said Allie simply when Harding wondered, aloud, how the fire was still alive. "It's what you asked for and got, isn't it?"

"I suppose," said Harding. None of this made sense and he was simply rolling with it now, rolling in the centre of the fever dream day. Allie handed him a pebble and a sharpie and said, "Write a new wish."

"What should I write?"

Allie didn't reply, simply looked at him with what they had both taken to calling *the stare,* the look that said, *Don't be an idiot.* "Oh, yeah," he said, smiling despite everything, and scribbled over the pebble. Using a stick, he knocked a hole into the heart of the remaining fire and pushed the pebble in, covering it even as its surface was blackening and heating. They waited, holding hands, Harding looking helplessly around him at the trees and the shadows and hearing the approaching noises again even as Allie said, "There's nothing there."

"No?"

"No. Trust me."

"I do."

"Good. It's time." Allie went to the fire and dug into it, using the same stick Harding had, dragging the stone to the edge of the pit and up the small wall much as she had the other night, then forcing it into the mud. A tiny curl of steam rose from it and a sweet, earthy smell. They waited another minute then Allie dug the stone from the earth, handing it to Harding who put it into his pocket. He kept his hand around it for a second, trying to feel through its covering of ash and mud whether the words were still on its surface even as he knew it was pointless; all he felt was grit and the slimy residue of burning.

The way back was worse. Whilst they had been up on the hillside, the streets had filled and now the bugs were moving among the dead. Here and there were small grey aliens, eyes large, although Harding didn't remember seeing children dressed up as aliens on Halloween night. Perhaps they had been there and he'd seen them without seeing them, he thought, the same as he must have seen children dressed as clowns because there were clowns on the streets as well, painted grins wide on faces that looked to have melted and bubbled and dripping down to create elongated masks that didn't quite hide the tombstone teeth that filled their mouths. Allie and Harding went along back streets, ducking behind walls when they needed to, once crouching behind a car as a cluster of the dead moved along the centre of the road and all the while people on the pavements and in cars saw nothing, moved out of the way or slowed down without apparently realising it, and Halloween bloomed again.

Allie's parents were out, thankfully, so they went straight to the bathroom. In the harsh light Harding's face looked pale in the mirror and Allie's looked worse, wan and curdled like old milk. He took the stone from his pocket and ran it under the tap, washing away the mud and ash. He thought about doing this the other night, the two of them in their underwear and happy, thought about the night they'd had and the time they'd had since, and wished they could go back.

The letters were still on the stone, a wish left ungranted.

"Oh," said Allie from behind him as Harding stared down at the stone in his hand, her voice suddenly choking off in disappointment. He watched the water run over the stone and his finger, rivulets spilling into the sink, crawling this way and that and glittering, and then he remembered. He lifted his face, looking at Allie in the mirror as she became the drowned ghost girl, her eyes rolling back and her hair soaking into rats' tail twists, and when the black water spilled from her mouth and spattered down her chin he screamed and screamed.

And then it was Halloween forever.

AFTERWORD

THERE ARE MOMENTS in life; they're not incendiary, they're not grand, they don't make you gasp or weep or see the world from a new angle. They're tiny, fragments of other things and times, little leaps of faith or conversation, unimportant at the time. They go mostly unnoticed, just part of the flow, but if you're lucky they can become critical afterwards, gathering a thickening strata of vitality the further forward you travel from them in time. This book is a result of one of those moments, and it happened like this:

I'm travelling home from launching my first book, *Lost Places*, at the World Horror Convention in Brighton in 2010 ("joining the Shakespeare club" my friend and eminent philosopher Steve Duffy calls it), and I've had a great time. I've been with people I like, love and genuinely admire, I've been drunk, hungover and sober, I've had the second most embarrassing photograph taken of me ever (don't ask about the first), I've signed books and bought books, I've been woken by seagulls walking across the skylight of my room in the early hours of the morning, I've made new friends, seen old ones and eaten doughnuts on the pier with my wife. And I've written a book, and it's been published and people seem to like it.

The question is, of course, what next? I have enough stories for a second collection, I think, and ideas for more, but I'm unsure of where to go or who to speak to about it. I'm muttering and moaning about this when the afore-mentioned Mr Duffy, great sage and clearly no lover of my muttering, says, "Why don't you pitch it to PS?"

"Okay," I said, "I will." And I did, several days later, and instead of turning me down like I expected them to, they said yes and here we are.

When I came to choose which stories to send to PS, hoping that they might like them, I started to think about the strange links that exist between the apparently separate tales I'd produced. Each individual story seems to have a thematic mirror in one of the others I was considering sending, creating a set of weird doubles (and one triple; more on that later). The linking factors were, mostly, my own obsessions and concerns and the various arcane and sidelong ways I tend to interpret the world, but they were there, and suddenly the collection began to have a structure in my head.

I should point out here that I'm not going to tell you what the themes are, because I have no urge to predispose you to a particular interpretation of any of the stories, and also because the few people I have mentioned them to have tended to look blankly at me and say, "No, sorry, can't see what you mean." See them or not, recognise the same concerns or not, though, it doesn't matter; I know they're there, all of the little tensions and joys and engines of my existence, filtered through the lenses of ghosts and demons and really, *really* bad days. *Strange Gateways*, once I let the themes play themselves out (purely imaginary though they may be), pretty much structured itself, and you can't say better than that, I don't suppose.

These stories were written in a variety of places, at a variety of times; on trains staring at the shifting landscapes of England as I went from one work venue to another, in my lounge and bedroom, sitting at my garden table on a beautiful summer's night drinking a beer and working to a suddenly tightened deadline and once on a plane at some godforsaken height flying to Calgary and with raging insomnia. Some were written to commission, some because I felt like it and one or two because the stories themselves left me no choice. All posed their own unique problems (writing about Zambia having never been there, for example, or writing a pulp 'creature feature' horror story having never written one before and knowing that my style doesn't lend itself easily to fast-paced narratives because I'm by nature a slow, wordy writer, to name a couple of examples), but all were fun to create and I don't remember any fighting me that badly. They were all made to stand alone and to fall or die on their own merits, but somehow between them they made a (to me, at least) pleasing whole.

A word about the title—I've come to realise that I like geographies, things that tie me strongly to environments. I like a sense of place and of where I am, and what I like about horror stories is that, at their best, they disrupt the sense of having an understood space in the world around you. The absolute best horror tales (King's or Klein's or James') paint a brilliantly realised world, place you into it, and then tilt it sideways so that you slip and scrabble and lose your grip, letting you plummet to somewhere entirely new yet awfully, horribly familiar, one step and a whole existence away from the world you know and trust. My first collection was called *Lost Places* because the stories in it were mostly about the places we slip into; this one is called *Strange Gateways* because, if there's an obvious thread between all the tales it contains, it's that they seem to me to represent the moment where we start to step from one place to another. There are no creaking doors, I don't think, no signs to give us warning, just sudden twists and shifts.

Just gateways, and the things that lie beyond them.

STORY NOTES

MORRIS EXPEDITION, DAYS NINE AND TEN

I LIKE PULP FICTION (not the Tarantino movie, although I do, I mean the genre), so when I was offered the chance to write a pulp fiction creature feature story (for an anthology called, excitingly, *Creature Feature*), I jumped at the chance. I duly wrote and submitted the story ('Implementing the Least Desirable Solution', more about it later), thoroughly enjoying what was, for me, a completely new genre of writing, and was delighted when the publisher liked it and asked if I'd consider writing a couple of smaller stories for the anthology. I agreed, on one condition (absolute arrogance, I realise, but if you don't ask you don't get)—that I be allowed to write stories that acted as essentially a prologue and an epilogue to the story I'd already sent him. They'd be standalone tales but linked, I told him, and would create (I hoped) something dramatic and cinematic and thrilling in three parts. Okay, he said, with a remarkable degree of trust in me...

What I wanted to do over the three stories was present a story that fulfilled its pulp remit, was fast and violent and managed to capture some of the essence of the creature features I'd grown up reading and loving. Guy N. Smith's *Crabs* books were a key reference point if you're interested, as were a raft of truly terrible but terribly fun 'revenge nature' novels about scorpions, worms, spiders, locusts and once, memorably, the unassuming and entirely harmless bug nicknamed the Devil's Coachhorse. The spirit of the marvellous James Herbert's early work cannot be under-estimated, as well as those fifties sci-fi horrors, giant creatures scouring across the landscape, and their seventies post-*Jaws* reappearance in garish technicolour, all of it filtered through my own sensibilities. I wanted to try something a little more ambitious, though—to try to write a pulp three-parter that ultimately reinforced my belief that horror isn't so much about the physical as it is the emotional, and I therefore tried to be a little more honest about people's emotional responses to those situations. There's something elemental and truly terrifying about stories in which we're attacked by, essentially, bloody great eating machines equipped with claws or teeth or poisons and ferocious appetites, because we're so powerless in the face of them, and I can't help but love them and wanted to explore, a little, what being in that kind of situation might mean.

This prologue story, then, is the pre-credits sequence, setting up the chaos to come and is dedicated to everyone who's prepared to step further into the jungle...

F BOMB

I'm fairly sure that this story came about because of a comment on Facebook.

Now, you have to understand, I swear. A lot. I *love* foul

language, the more creative and odder the better; I'm not talking here about simple insults or crudities, but that point where the foulness becomes almost poetry, lifting itself above the lumpen weight of mere bad language. Helen Grant (the author, incidentally, of a number of excellent ghost stories and several genuinely magnificent young adult thrillers) upbraided me for dropping the 'F Bomb' into something I'd said on Facebook, which made me stop for a minute. I'd never heard the phrase 'F Bomb' before and it made me laugh, and then (as these things often do) started me thinking. I drop the F Bomb all the time, lots of people do, and it's being reduced in its power to shock or emphasise (which I think is a shame, if I'm honest, although I do realise I'm contributing to this diminution). How, I wondered, could the F Bomb regain its power? Under what circumstances? When, I decided, it ceased to be a choice and became a helpless, hopeless thing. What would that feel like? What would it lead to? And this story is the result, and it is dedicated in its entirety to Helen, with grateful thanks that she has better linguistic standards than I do and stands up for her beliefs.

THE HOTEL GUEST

A story based entirely on the behaviour of the lifts in the notorious Britannia Hotel, Nottingham. I had gone there for my first British Fantasy Society Convention (FantasyCon, for those in the know, or even FCon if you're feeling really confident). I had a truly great time there . . . except for the lifts. Sometimes they didn't come when called. Sometimes they came and then refused to move any further. Sometimes, they went to floors whose button no one had pushed. They lurched, they rocked, they acted like sulking teenagers, and I suddenly thought, What if one day they don't just go to the wrong floor, but the wrong *place*? To the wrong hotel, or a wrong version of the right hotel? And what would I find there if I didn't realise and had walked out of the lifts and had the doors close behind me before I could stop them?

My initial thought was to have a nice, normal hero battling weird alternate-universe Lovecrafty beasties, but even as I started to write it, I knew it wasn't working. It seemed much more interesting to have something quieter happening, something no less grotesque but less obvious, and to have a hero who was actually a complete shit. I wondered about infections, and inflammations and what happens to people who disappear, and "The Hotel Guest" is what emerged. Incidentally, I went back to the Nottingham Britannia the year after, again for FCon, and the lifts were, if anything, worse.

This story is dedicated to editor of taste, style and distinction Stephen Jones, without whose encouragement I'd never have gone to FCon in the first place, never met all the authors and editors and artists whom I'm now proud to call friends, and never met the Britannia lifts...

THE KNITTED CHILD

My son was conceived using IVF.

I say this not to generate sympathy or awe, but to explain this story. After a first, unsuccessful attempt which exhausted us (Wendy and I had to travel from Lancaster to Manchester, Wendy more than I, often early in the morning), we decided to stay with my grandparents for our second attempt, because they lived near the clinic. IVF, for those of you who don't know, is hard; there's lots of drugs to cope with, emotional ups and downs, and there's no guarantee of success, and the second go was no easier than the first. One night, both of us knackered, we were talking with my grandparents (the wonderful Hazel, and Barry, the most important and influential man in my life after my dad) and my grandma made some passing comment that if it didn't work this time, she'd knit us a baby. It was one of those jokes that made us laugh even as we felt a bit weird about it, and later that night I lay in bed and wondered ... If a child was knitted into existence, how would it feel?

I actually didn't write the story straight away (it felt a bit raw), but tackled it a year or so later. I stepped away from my usual style and tried when writing it to find a tone of magical realism (more than anything because it provided a distance between me and the subject matter I was writing about, letting me treat the story as almost a technical exercise rather a direct attempt to harness my more normal emotional horrors), finally ending up with a story that I think is both almost fairy tale in tone and as bleak as anything I've written. It is, of course, dedicated to my grandparents, Hazel and Barry, who gave me the original idea and whose support and love and advice and hospitality and jokes I have been lucky enough to experience for the whole of my forty years on earth. It is also dedicated to Wendy and Ben, who survived the ordeal of IVF and beyond, and without whom this story could not exist.

THE DRUNKS' TOTEM

Based on a true story. Sort of.

I run (well, kind of wheeze about the place whilst wearing white trainers that look like mutant Cornish pasties), and one of the times and places I run is early in the morning along a cycle racetrack by the river Lune. In summer, it's lovely; I see herons fishing and preening, gulls plunging into the water and I say hello to the other runners and dog walkers. In winter, however, it's bitter and dark and solitary. I sometimes take my dog with me, a black beast of cheerful temperament who runs around me and plays with any piece of litter he finds as I jog. One particular morning, I'd already spooked myself; it was misty and very cold and I'd put a LED collar on the dog and had thereafter been chased around the track by something that was little more than a shadow with glimmers of red flashing intermittently from it, which my imagination had already turned into all manner of silly things…and then I came upon the sculpture.

It was placed in the middle of the grassy section at the head of the circuit where it bends back upon itself in a shepherd's crook of a turn. It loomed out of the mist at me, tall and angular, and for a moment I was being attacked by every damned nightmare I'd ever had, by every creature I'd ever written about or watched in a movie or read about in stories and books. I know I screeched, I know I literally staggered away from it, slipping and losing my running rhythm, which my dog took as a sign that I really, really wanted to play and hurtled out of the mist and jumped on me and for one terrible instant I was living in my own stories and my heart was jolting and my belly was clenching and then I recognised the dog (mostly by his breath, it has to be said), and reality crashed back in.

Once I'd got the stupid animal off me, the nightmare thing had resolved itself into an odd construction of sticks and old wine and cider bottles made, I assume, by the drunks who often congregate at the cycle track and whose leavings I frequently found. I laughed at my silliness, and started to run again…and about two hundred yards down the track I had an image of a very fat man trying hard to better himself coming across the sculpture, and started to wonder what it might mean to him. Who had put it there, if not the drunks? And why? What gateway would it signify, I wondered, and what terrors might lie on the other side? And now I know.

This story is dedicated to my dog of little brain and unending cheeriness, Swayze, whose flashing red collar almost certainly primed me to see monsters where there were only drunken offerings. Thanks, boy, but please, stop jumping on me.

IMPLEMENTING THE LEAST DESIRABLE SOLUTION

Ah, monsters; I love 'em.

I'd sort of written monster stories prior to this one ("The Derwent Water Shark" and "Flappy the Bat" from *Lost Places* might conceivably be monster stories if you look at them from the right angle), but this was the first time I (encouraged by the editor of the *Creature Feature* anthology) set my pen (well, okay, my typing fingers) to write a full on monster story. "I want pulp," I told myself. "Things spurting and squashing and roaring and a minimum of characterisation and a maximum of blood!" And I started...and I couldn't do it, not quite. My own preferences for stories rooted in some kind of emotional reality meant I kept trying to understand my main character better, trying to work out where he'd come from and what drove him. I also couldn't help but make the creature just slightly supernatural. It was strange, something I've still not quite worked out, but in my head when I wrote this story (and the prologue and epilogue stories afterwards), I had a curious reference point— one of my favourite stories, "The Wendigo" by Algernon

Blackwood. I knew I wasn't up to writing a sequel but I stole some of his imagery to suggest the idea that my idiot scientists had somehow captured the terrible thing from his tale (or, more probably, the thing had allowed itself to be captured). Why riff off Blackwood? I don't know, other than that I wanted to and "The Wendigo" seems to me to be a great blend of mythology, monster horror and the supernatural, one of the best there is. This story isn't anything to do with Blackwood's, not really, but I see the little links to it, and it pleases me.

I also felt, by the time I finished it, that I'd managed to find enough of a downbeat, apocalyptic tone and ending so that I could feel sorry for my main character (who isn't a hero, no), allowing me to see him as a real human being without having to make him read as a nice person. I managed to cram in death, chaos, smoke, bloody great creature attacks, dismemberment, vomit and implied and extended threat; to be honest, that's all I look for from a creature feature, and I remain happy with it to this day.

A note: at the time I was writing the first versions of this, my mate Andrew was having a crap time at work. Meeting him for coffee one day, he seemed really down, but he perked up when I offered to kill his boss in the story. "There's two of them being horrible," he said. "No worries," I said, "I'll kill them both." We merged the two into one character and had the creature eat him and, to Andrew's delight and as a special surprise, had his remains being found in the creature's spoor. I mention this only to point out the power of the author, and to counsel you to beware—always be nice to writers, and buy them drinks, or terrible fates may befall you.

This story is dedicated to Andrew, who gave a character a name and told me he liked it when I killed that character. His smile was enough to make me think I'd done something good.

TRAFFIC STREAM

No idea where this came from, although one reviewer described it as apparently being a story about a giant, dangerous game of PacMan, which I liked. I think (I *think*) that this was just one of those stories that came simply from trying to work out what one of the weird images in my head (one about fishes that looked like cars and trucks chasing each other along desert roads) actually meant, and what preceded and came after the image. Originally I had hoped to do the whole thing as a dialogue in phone calls, but in the end I dropped that idea because it felt like I was constraining things with little reason.

There's not much else to say about "Traffic Stream" except this—the two characters in it are named after a couple of authors who got into an unpleasant spat following the 2009 FCon. I'm not going to go into the details of the argument, because you can find it easily enough if you're interested; it's all over various internet forums from the time, and I certainly blogged about it and expressed my opinion fairly clearly. The characters in the story aren't based on the individuals involved in any way except for their names; I simply did it to cheer up the author who I thought was being treated extremely shabbily and bullied by the other. I've been criticised for this; I don't give a fuck. Allyson Bird, this story is for you.

A MAN OF ICE AND SORROW

I don't quite know where this came from either, although I do remember talking to someone about writing an 'evil snowman' story and wondering what it would turn out like if I did. The answer is, of course, that the snowman wouldn't be evil and my main character would, as always, be struggling with horrors both internal and external. Mains (named for Johnny Mains, incidentally, the editor and proprietor of Noose and Gibbet Publishers and a stalwart fellow who has done much laudable work in bringing the *Pan Book of Horror Stories* back into the public eye, and to whom this story is dedicated for no reason other than I nicked his name because I couldn't think of another at the time of writing) is one of those characters dealing with traumas that I can't imagine ever having the strength to cope with. His miseries reflect my own fears of the time, I think, probably more closely than in anything else I've written.

Whether you believe it or not, I think this story has a happy ending.

MAMI WATI

This is one of the stories I'm proudest of.

When I got back from the World Fantasy Convention in Calgary in 2008, having had (at that point) two stories published, I was kind of wondering what to do next and whether I was a proper author or just a mild flash in the pan. I had story ideas, for sure, but had, at that point, more rejections than acceptances (way, way more). And then I got an email from Danel Olsen, who edits the extremely well-received *Exotic Gothic* series, published at that point by the Ash Tree Press and now by PS Publishing. "Write me a gothic themed story," he said, "but not set in traditional gothic landscapes."

"Okay," says I and, more for a laugh than anything, then said, "I'll set it in Zambia."

Why Zambia? Well, because I have a family friend lives

there, of course, and Africa isn't the traditional home of gothic literature. Besides, where else would you set a gothic-themed story that wasn't allowed to take place in the traditional environments of the gothic?

This story was my first proper commission, to rules set by other people that helped to shape and frame the tale, and I loved writing it. I did some actual proper research about Zambian mythology, asked my family friend (whose name I also stole for my main character—there's a recurring motif there, have you noticed?) lots of questions about mine workings and Zambian culture (and who patiently gave me all the information I wanted and more, despite the increasingly stupid questions I asked, and helped make the story much better in the process). It was also improved immeasurably after the first draft by both Danel's editorial suggestions and some of the additional details he found about Zambia, and by the feedback from the people I showed it to who were kind enough to email their thoughts to me.

What finally emerged managed, I think, to incorporate the best of my own peculiar obsessions around human inter-actions and frailties and desires as well as good old-fashioned supernatural threat and terror. It also taught me that I could use mythologies, giving me the confidence to add to them, bend them to the shapes I needed them to be, and in the process I created something that I liked and I thought other people might like too (a feeling which seems to be justified; "Mami Wata" was selected for reprinting in Stephen Jones' *The Mammoth Book of Best New Horror 21*, and reader feedback is generally positive).

Here's a weird thing about "Mami Wata", though—after it was done and submitted, I was talking to someone about it and mentioned that it was the first story I'd written in which my hero survived. "No they didn't," they replied, "he died."

"Thorley survives!" I said, thinking perhaps that this person hadn't read the story as closely as they'd claimed.

"Thorley isn't your hero," they said. "Chilongo is."

And you know what? They were dead right. It's still dedicated to the real Thorley (whose name, incidentally, is Barry), though, simply for the patience he showed me when I was trying to put this together and for the information he gave me about mines.

THE SEVEN PEOPLE YOU DON'T MEET TODAY

Another one based, in some ways, on a completely real incident.

I have, for a long time, loved stories in which one world is discovered to be lurking within the confines of another, out of sight but subtly manipulating and controlling and encroaching upon its host (T.E.D. Klein's "Children of the Kingdom" or "The Events at Poroth Farm" being perfect examples, and if you've not read them, why not?), but had never written one because I'd never had quite the right inspiration or been confident enough in my skills to manage it. And then a bloke nodded at me in the centre of town one Saturday afternoon, and by that night the story was in my head almost fully formed.

Perhaps I should explain. When the bloke nodded at me, it was a definite, *I know you, hello fellah!* nod, not a friendly stranger nod. The problem was, I didn't know him. I spent the next few hours trying to think who he was, this guy in a T shirt and jeans who clearly knew me, and it was only as I had my first beer of the evening that I suddenly recognised him; I normally saw him when he was wearing a suit, standing at a train platform.

He was a commuter buddy!

I'm not explaining this well, I am? Each morning, I'd walk a mile and a half to the train station to go to work, and I realised when I thought about it that I was part of a little community of people who knew each other only by sight, who passed each other at roughly the same places each day or sat near each other. We never spoke, didn't know each other's names, but still, I wondered where they were if I didn't see them, and took an odd kind of reassurance from their presence. They were little markers on my journey, and I enjoyed their existence, and I started to wonder, what if not just one was missing or running late, what if they all vanished one by one? What would happen to the rest of my life if these little supports that I hadn't even realised mattered to me were removed? And from such tiny beginnings . . . All of the people in this story are the real ones I saw on that walk every morning, and it is to them that this tale is dedicated.

One last little thing—the title of this story came about because I don't like self-help books. I mean, I can see how they're incredibly useful, but they somehow never quite connect with me; it's probably a failing in my personality rather than in the books themselves, but there you go. As I was writing "The Seven People You Don't Meet Today", I started to think that I'd uncovered some great truth about the human condition, and there was probably a self-help book there, helping people to recognise the entirely unexpected structures we gather to ourselves. The book, I thought, would help us to recognise them, to understand their importance to the functioning of our lives, and giving us the capacity to cope with it if they changed or disappeared. I'm not the man to write that book, though; instead, I wrote a story with a slightly sarcastic title about a man losing any semblance of control he might once have had. Again, this is probably a failing in me, but it's not one I'm going to worry about.

PEEK A BOO

I can't escape who I am and, as I may have said, I've always cared more about the emotional impact of horror than the physical or practical ones. Having had a huge amount of fun writing the first two pulp stories for *Creature Feature*, I knew that the third piece had to provide a kind of ending but also had to explore what it might *feel* like to experience something like that; not physically, that's just pain, but what emotions it might conjure up, what terrors, and what impact it might have on the people involved. I wanted to write something that both pointed out the problem with pulp fictions (the worst of them often completely ignore the emotional elements of horror) but that also stayed firmly within the pulp 'rules' (as I understood them, at least), and that also showed how good pulp can have it both ways. I still needed a creature attack, of course, and death and bloodshed, but I wanted to try to write about what this might *mean* to the characters involved, to have them react as realistically as possible, to be as believable (and therefore as easy to relate to) as I could make them.

I made the main character a child because, of course, it's far worse to imagine this happening to the innocents, and at the end of the day I wanted to upset my readers as much as possible. Whether I achieved any of the aims I set myself, I don't know, but taken as a triumvirate I like these stories and think they work well together, and they're dedicated to every pulp author whose books I loved and whose stories made my brain soar and my imagination leap. You have my thanks, and gratitude.

—Simon Kurt Unsworth
Somewhere on a train, September 2012

ACKNOWLEDGEMENTS

THIS IS AN interesting one, this question of who to thank. This collection was the second one I pitched and sold, but because of the way publishing works, it's actually the third I've had published and none of the stories in it were written more recently than a couple of years ago. So, do I do my thanks for the people back then, or the people now? Or mix them all up and do the lot? As ever, I suspect I'll make it up as I go along.

Anyway, these people have my gratitude (and possibly deserve medals):

Wendy and Benjamin, who spent the time I wrote these stories putting up with me despite all my major provocations and failings, and without whom these stories would not exist, or if they did, would exist in very different forms.

Pete and Nicky Crowther at PS, who took a chance on a relatively unknown author and said they'd publish his collection, despite the thoroughly odd pitch he sent them.

Family, of course—all of them. I have too big a family to name them individually, but they know who they are.

Steve Marsh, still a Krautrock-loving barrister and all-round best mate this particular author has got.

Andrew Worgan, just because he's my other best mate and my nights on the whisky with him are among the most enjoyable times I spend, just talking crap and laughing so hard it often makes my stomach ache.

Every editor who's agreed to publish my work and then helped me improve it: Barbara Roden, Stephen Jones, Danel Olsen, Charles Prepolec and Jeff Campbell, Ellen Datlow, Simon Marshall-Jones, Richard Salter, John Prescott, Charles Black, Gary Fry, Joel Lane and Allyson Bird, Paul Finch, Peter Mark May and Mike Davis. May there be many more of you in the future!

The Monkeyrack crew, still the best writing comrades there are: Mollie Baxter, Norman Hadley, Sarah Fiske, Ron Baker, Rachel McGladdery, Vickie Ellis, Angela Norman and our honorary member, the alternately sleepy or grumpy Ted. Long may we continue to search for a decent venue to meet in, Lords and Ladies.

The critical circle—Chris Thompson, Barry Thorley, Paul Buschini, Glyn Mottershead, Huw Lines, Will Mansell and Karen Monk and all the others. Keep the feedback coming!

Jason van Hollander for his excellent covers, which make my work look much better than it deserves.

The mighty Bellowhead, who made me realise that folk music is really rather cool.

The Bad Shepherds, just because.

Mike Harding, folk music DJ and comedian, bigger influence on me in two completely separate areas of my life, three decades apart, than he will ever know, and provider of the best description of Cameron's 'Big Society' that I have ever heard.

There are a lot of authors I consider to be not just

influences but also friends, and who I need to thank for both their time and their friendship. So, in no real order, thanks are due to Stephen Volk (pastries and coffee in Soho never tasted so good!), David Hutchinson (write another book! Now!), Laurence C. Connolly (author, musician and all-round lovely bloke), John L. Probert (gleeful purveyor of fiction far smarter than it first appears to be), Thana Niveau (puts up with me being too damned noisy in signing sessions), Mark Morris (thinks he's got me beaten on the garish shirts front, but is sadly mistaken), Paul Finch (writes both books and movies; I'm not jealous, no, not me), Gary McMahon (apparently the angriest man ever, until you meet him in person and you realise he's a big softie), Simon Bestwick (Salford lad with an airship fixation), Graham Joyce (too damn talented), Rob Shearman (funnier than almost everyone else I've met, and also too damn talented), Sarah Pinborough (smart, sharp, makes me dance at discos, swears more than anyone else I've ever met and is alarmingly lovely in person), Reggie Oliver (best voice ever), Robert Lloyd Parry (actor, writer, and all-round fabulous bloke), Brian J. Showers (takes photographs of my knees for some reason), Ramsey Campbell (the Godfather), Dave Jeffrey (ever show that film of me dancing to anyone and this is the last acknowledgement you'll get from me, fellah), Helen Grant (write another ghost story please), Jo Baker (fellow Lancaster Café Nero refugee) and Alison Littlewood (go and read her books, now).

There are definitely others that I've forgotten; apologies, but my memory is deteriorating as I get older. You hopefully know who you are.

Everyone above has contributed to my life and my wellbeing and to my writing in ways they may know or might guess or might be entirely unaware of, and clearly what I've produced is in some way their responsibility so you can blame them and not me.

For what it's worth, however, this book is dedicated to one person—the beautiful, wonderful and quite magnificent Rosie. Without your light and life and influence, I'd be in a far worse place than I am now, and be a far more shrunken and shrivelled person. You are the beginning and the end and the middle, and there's a moment in the sun on a slope outside a café that will live in my heart and my memory forever and will always make me realise just how special life can be. This is for you, my sweet, with all the love I can muster and all the thanks I'm capable of generating. Without you, I'd be lost.